The Galactic Empire Wants You!

The Galactic Empire Wants You!

Marshall Pickens

Corvid Publishing

This is a work of fiction. All characters, organizations, and events portrayed in this novel are either products of the author's imagination or are used fictitiously.

The Galactic Empire Wants You!

Copyright 2022 by Marshall Pickens

This goes out to all the help I've had
from great friends like Benjamin Schwarting (buy his books too)
and locations like Jitters in Eagle River Alaska
that let me take up a table in the corner to write.
Also, and especially, to Liam for the use of Sockman.
Thank you.

Chapter: Will

"Hurry," Will muttered, "Come on, stupid door, I know you're automatic." He waved his arms around in the hope it would trigger whatever was needed to get the door to open. All the ones before this, including the door to his room, or cell, or whatever he'd woken up in, had opened when he'd walked up to them. In some cases, ran up to them would be the more appropriate phrase.

Looking over his shoulder, he knew the guards would show up around the corner any moment. He assumed they were guards for many reasons which he didn't have time to think about. Now, if the door would just open. What currently blocked his path was a rectangular piece of gray metal, and if it functioned the same as all the others it should slide back into the wall without a sound. In fact, the entire set of doors and hallways all seemed to be made of metal. It all looked polished and antiseptic, like what he imagined the tables were made of in morgues. All the dead bodies laid out ready for dissection with some cop leaning over them trying to figure out who killed them. In his case it was going to be the guards.

They might be robots, he thought. They didn't say anything, and you couldn't see anything on them that would lead you to believe they weren't robots. Granted he'd never seen any robots that ran on two legs and moved like a person, but this had been a day just chock full of things he'd never seen, so he couldn't put much stock in his previous opinions right now.

"Open!" He slammed the side of his closed fist against the door and froze for a moment. It wasn't the sound of flesh hitting metal that stopped him, the guards already knew where he was, it was the dent.

Looking from his hand to the door he realized his options were very limited at that point. He didn't really relish the thought of slamming himself into a solid door, but he couldn't exactly MacGyver his way out of this. For starters, he didn't have anything to work with. The hallway was empty. Just a sleek metal corridor broken every once in a while by a sliding door, which at this moment didn't seem to want to cooperate. His clothes had been taken when he was unconscious and replaced by a white robe with no pockets. Thankfully they'd left his boxers. Hopefully his Superman boxers were a good omen.

Shrugging in resignation and with no time left, he took a step back, and decided he'd rather try kicking it than throwing his shoulder into it. Theoretically it should hurt less, or so he hoped. Picturing all the police shows he'd watched he stepped up and kicked at the middle of the door with all the force he could muster.

With a screeching sound like a muffler dragging behind a speeding car the door buckled and tumbled down the hallway. Shocked Will looked from the imprint left on the still sliding door to his own unshod foot. With no shoes to go along with the white robe he'd expected the kick to hurt, but no.

Not wanting to waste the moment, and hearing noises from behind him, he took off down the newly opened corridor. He briefly thought of grabbing the broken door and using it somehow against his silent pursuers, but not really having a plan he decided to run until something presented itself.

Will's bare feet slapped at the tightly woven industrial gray carpet as he took turns at random. He had no idea if there was surveillance of any kind, so he wasn't really sure if his twists and turns were helping him, but he did know they weren't hurting. He didn't need to worry about getting lost since he had no idea where he was to begin with, having woken up in a room wearing this plain robe with only the vaguest idea of how he'd gotten there.

His thoughts were interrupted as he came to a crossroads and saw two guards running toward the same intersection from the hallway on the left. Will put his hand out and used the intersecting corner to break himself, then put his foot up on the wall and pushed off to head back the way he'd come. Glancing over his shoulder, he saw where he'd left multiple dents in the wall from his quick turn around. At the same time movement caught his eye from the opposite hallway, and he groaned thinking he was going to have even more of the silent goon squad on his tail.

He was shocked when two figures dressed in white robes ran from the intersecting hallway. A man running in front of a darker skinned woman stretched out his arms and football tackled the two guards who were focused on Will. The guards left their feet and flew a very short distance with a sudden stop at the opposite wall. They would have collapsed to the floor if they hadn't been jammed into the indents now left by their massive collision with what Will had thought was a solid wall.

Realizing he'd stopped running and was just staring, open mouthed, he made the split second decision to not start running again. These were the first normal people he'd seen since he escaped from his cell.

"Do you think they're the same ones?" Will twitched when the guy spoke up.

The girl bent over and looked at the unmoving guards, "There's really no way to tell. I'm not really convinced there were ever more than two of them to begin with."

Will watched them. They seemed to know each other from the way they were interacting. One was a girl of, what Will's brain would classify as asian descent. Dark straight hair was pulled back and tied in a ponytail with what looked like a strip of cloth torn from her robe. She was easily shorter than his six feet two inches, but at this distance and with no distinguishing marks on the walls to use as a gauge he could only guess she was somewhere under five and a half feet tall. Her skin wasn't a black coffee, but more like someone added some cream to it to bring it down a shade or two. Her eyes, however, had no cream added and were so brown they could almost be classified as black.

Next to her was a brick of a guy. He was only slightly taller than the girl and sported messy light brown hair, and other than his dense build was almost as average as a person could get. Will revised that thought because, he said to himself, average really depends on where you came from. Will came from Idaho; rampant with potatoes, white people, and farm equipment. This guy would fit right in. In fact he looked like he would be a perfect lineman for a local high school football team. A good brick in the wall.

He wasn't quite sure what was going on, but more people to work with was always a good thing, so he walked up to them with his hand extended. "Hey, I'm Will, thanks for the assist."

The guy shook Will's hand, "My name's Ron, and this is…" He looked over at his female companion.

Turning to Will she also extended her hand, "I'm Mai Lee Thao, but you can call me Mai, and just in case you're like Ron here, I'll answer the question before you ask. I'm from Thailand, or I should say my parents are from Thailand. I'm from Seattle."

Will nodded and shook her hand, "I had a few Thao's in classes I taught."

"Oh," Mai looked sideways at Ron, "a teacher. An educated man. A man who can make better arguments than, I'm not going to follow the line because that's what they want me to do."

Will chuckled, "To be honest, that is why they were chasing me." He remembered the voice in the cell telling him to exit the room and follow the line to the processing station. The door had slid open and a glowing red line had lit up on the floor heading off to the left. "I grew up around cattle farms and slaughterhouses. When they said I was going to be processed…" He shrugged and left the thought hanging there.

Ron nodded vigorously, "It's like that old Twilight Zone episode called 'To Serve Man' where they're all nice but it turns out they just want to eat us."

"I still think following the line would have kept us safer than bringing security down on us," Mai said. "We needed to know what was going on with the aliens before we tried to do anything."

Aliens. The word popped into Will's mind. We're standing here, in what might be a space ship, talking about aliens. shaking his head he decided he really didn't need to be distracted right now. Getting away, or something, was more important.

"How did you two know you could take the guards out like that?" Will looked over to the still unmoving guards.

"Before we answer that," Mai said, "how bout we move along in case they decide to reboot, or wake up, or whatever."

Will nodded, she was right, but before he could say anything Ron pointed down one of the hallways and said, "That way."

"Why that way?" Will asked as they headed down the hall. He really didn't care which way they went since he hadn't been keeping track during his panicked getaway attempt.

Ron tapped his head, "I've been keeping track of the turns and doors."

Will looked at Mai who just shrugged and gave him a look that said, I don't know any more than you do.

"What?" Ron looked at the two of them, "I like math."

Ron dialed the pace up from a walk to a jog and said, "I have no idea what the layout of this place is, but I figure if we keep moving away from the red line, and away from the cells we came out of, we should find something."

"It's a better plan than I had." Will said.

Ron glanced over at him, "What was your plan?"

"Run." Will answered.

A door to their right slid open and two more guards jumped through and into the hallway. Without breaking stride Will lowered his shoulder and hockey style body checked the leftmost guard while Ron jumped and kicked the other in the center of his reflective face mask. Both guards tumbled down the hallway while the three of them bounded over and away from them.

8

Will understood now why Ron ended up confused and wasn't sure if there were multiple guards or just two chasing them over and over through this maze of identical corridors. The two Ron and Mai had tackled back at the intersection looked exactly like the two they'd just run over. Both groups were in identical white body armor with blue trim. The armor seemed to lock together from the boots all the way to the fully sealed helmet. There was a reflective face mask of sorts that made a fat T shape, but Will wasn't sure if there was someone looking out from behind it or if it was just the camera piece of some humanoid robot.

"Door!" Ron pointed unnecessarily down the hall as they all watched the door slide shut in front of them.

"Kick it!" Will yelled, and when Ron gave him an are you crazy look, he took the lead and planted his size eleven foot directly in the middle of the offending door.

Ron let out a woop and fist pumped his way past Will who'd been slowed down by the impact. "Yesterday, I was worried I'd have to get a job at a fast food place, and today I'm Superman."

"You?" Mai shot him a look, "Will kicked the door down."

"True," Ron grinned at her, "but he told me I could, and then he did, which means I could. The force that would take is amazing. You would, of course, need to figure out the tensile strength of the metal, and then do some..."

"Guards!" Mai's shout cut Ron off mid sentence.

Will wasn't worried, and in fact he was feeling every bit the superman Ron had just claimed to be. Since waking up he'd kicked down two solid metal doors and tackled a guard, who may or may not be a robot, without even breaking a sweat. Come to think of it, they'd been running flat out for a good ten minutes now and he wasn't even breathing hard.

"No worries," Ron shot back, "remember, we have been improved!"

That statement crashed into Will's head and he remembered. He'd jerked awake and through the fog in his brain couldn't remember where he was and how he'd gotten there. It had pissed him off. Too many times he'd chided characters in movies or books for doing just that. How, he wondered, did a person ever wake up and just not know what was going on. Then, there he was, staring up at an alien ceiling with light slowly getting brighter and no idea of anything. Moving as little as possible, on the assumption that bad things might happen, he'd tried to take in his surroundings. The walls reminded him of aluminum, and the ceiling was all a dim blue white glow. Trying to look around without turning his head he felt a movement and realized the surface he was laying on had started to recede into the wall it was attached to.

Not wanting to tumble unceremoniously onto the floor, because, again, he was assuming bad things might happen, he instead slid off and into a crouch. He was hoping to make as small a target as possible for whatever horrible monstrosity was going to try and eat him. To his relief and slight consternation there was nothing in the room with him. The room was maybe ten feet by ten feet with a closed sliding door across from him. Looking down at himself he realized his clothes were gone and he'd been dressed in some kind of white robe. Shifting his weight he did note his boxer shorts were still in place.

The world around him began to feel very far away with the edges of his vision blurring. The floor felt like it was starting to tilt and his stomach began trying to send things back up. Waking up in a strange metal room, his clothes gone, and not knowing anything about how he'd gotten here or even where…

Taking a deep breath he decided fainting for the first time in his life wasn't going to help, and since there was no immediate threat he sat down and began taking deep breaths. He'd just gotten his stomach to listen to him and settle when a voice, which immediately reminded him of his brothers car navigation system, broke into the silence of his aluminum room.

"Welcome, and we thank you for your participation. Now that you have been improved, we would like you to proceed to processing. Please exit the room and follow the red line."

The door slid open revealing the first of many hallways he would soon see, except this one had a glowing red line on the floor, heading to the left. He assumed it was this he was supposed to follow to processing, but that wasn't going to happen. It wasn't really a thought out decision, but more of an instantaneous gut reaction. He wasn't going anywhere to be processed, so poking his head out the door and seeing no one he went right.

Now, with Ron's war cry echoing down the hallway and through his head, he knew what they meant when they said improved. He gained what he sincerely hoped was a wicked grin and charged the two identical guards. There had been times during his only year of teaching that he'd wished for super powers. To be fair the one power he'd actually wished for was time manipulation. Grading homework just took so long.

Will smiled as he watched the reflection of his fist connect with the face mask of the first guard. As a crack split the reflective surface a noise behind him caught his attention. Turning he watched as four guards entered the hallway, two each from opposite doors. Riffles snapped up and Will did the only thing he could think of.

Kicking his leg out he tripped Mai as she ran past him. Tumbling she slammed into Ron, knocking him to the ground. At the same time he simply went limp and dropped to the ground. Wondering if he would be able to see the red and blue lasers as they zapped their way over his head, he decided sitting still would just give them a better target so as he hit the floor he pushed off the wall and rolled to the left. On his back he was just in time to see Mai fly over him, followed by the solid thunk of person hitting person. Will wondered how long Ron was going to live after this fight was over. If they survived, he was fairly sure Mai was going to kill him for that little stunt.

Sitting up he saw three of the guards sprawled out with Main on top of one raising her fist. Ron ran past him yelling, "Sorry, it was the only thing I could think of…"

Getting to his feet, Will again heard the sliding of a door and pushing himself off the left wall spun to face two more guards entering the hallway. Picking up speed he pushed off the nearest wall to, hopefully, mess up their aim. This brought him to the first guard at an angle, and with the added speed his cross punch had enough force to launch the guard off the ground and into a beautiful pirouette. There was a sense of joy in it all. The speed of movement. The strength of the blow. Then the world went white, and pain flashed from his right side up and down his body. Muscles locked, and his jaw tightened so quickly his teeth audibly clacked together.

With loss of control he crashed into the wall and slid down. A white gloved hand with blue trim closed over his arm and flipped him over. Looking up into the mirrored visor all he could see was himself as the guard extended a rod.

Chapter: Ron

Ron decided he didn't like being knocked out. He guessed he couldn't really call it being knocked out since they didn't hit him with anything, so maybe blacking out would be more appropriate. Either way, they'd done it, and he didn't like it. He'd never blacked out before, not even when he'd broken his arm.

It had been a great play. Normally he didn't play defense, but the starting defensive end was out sick and there he was. It had been snowing off and on, making the ground muddy and slick. Granted it wasn't really the snow's fault for that. His podunk little high school didn't exactly have the best football field. The track circling it was dirt and required massive spikes for anyone on the track team. Halfway through the game he'd decided he liked defense better than offense. You didn't have to remember plays and you didn't have to fall back. All you did was attack and find ways of getting around the other guy. It made it much more of a chess game and Ron had loved it. It was math, but in a totally physical realm. Normally he dealt with graphs and equations, it was his happy place, but tonight he took the place of the X and the quarterback was the Y. All he had to do was figure out the best way to get from his starting point to where the ball was.

That was until he got a bit overzealous and decided he could take on the lineman and the running back at the same time. On the positive side, he'd managed a great tackle. On the negative side was the pop he'd heard from his arm as they landed on him.

His brother had to take him to the emergency room since their parents were out of town. When the doctor asked him to straighten his arm so they could get the football pads off the world had gotten very small. It was like looking down a very long dark tunnel with just a pin prick of light at the end, but he'd managed to keep it together.

This situation was different. They'd tapped him with some kind of knock out rod. Yes, that's what he was going to call it. Mai would give him that look like he was acting childish, but you know what, sometimes you have to call things like you see them, and in this case it was a knock out rod. They touched him with it and boom, out went the lights.

When he'd come to, he was sitting in a seriously uncomfortable gray plastic chair next to Will and Mai. The crazy thing was that it wasn't like waking up. Consciousness didn't slowly come back with the awareness that something had happened or changed.

Nope, one moment he was off and the next he was on. It was like someone had flipped a light switch, except it was a Ron switch. The really creepy thing, among all the other odd things he admitted to himself, was he'd woken up sitting perfectly. He wasn't slumped over or laying in the chair like the guards had dropped him there.

Anyway, he thought, something's obviously about to happen. He turned to Will, "What do you think's going to happen?" Sure, Will had just woken up too, but he'd mentioned being a teacher so he had to know more than Ron did.

"Well," Ron watched Will look around and realized he hadn't really taken the time to figure out where they were, "I would guess this is Processing."

"That," Mai said from the other side of Will, "could mean anything."

The room was exactly what Ron defined as stark. The walls were bare and stark white with a touch of reflectivity to them. It was a color that brought teeth to mind. The panels of the walls a ghastly rictus smiling at him. Walls the color of teeth? Ron's mind tried to pull away from the absurdity of the thought. Who would say that? Also, he continued to look around, the designers, whoever they were, didn't seem to care about color choices did they. And who were they? I mean, if they were aliens they still could have done better with their interior design choices. Even aliens need a nice work environment. Those hallways back there had been seriously utilitarian, and why was he, all of a sudden so obsessed with the design choices of alien kidnappers? At least these walls weren't metal, he thought. That would have just been overkill. On the other hand metal walls and floors do make clean up easier, which could mean they weren't planning on killing them here. Or if they were it would be a clean death. Other than the stark walls, there was that word stark again he thought, the overwhelming feature was the dozens of cloth partitioned booths with people being shoved into them by rod wielding guards. In fact, it mostly reminded him of the shots you see on the news of a gym at a local university after it had taken in refugees from some natural disaster. Aside from the rod wielding guards. Normally you didn't see space age armor wearing guards pushing people around with knockout rods after an earthquake had leveled your town. Unless the earthquake was caused by the aliens, or monsters. That would be a pretty cliche godzilla movie though.

Ron heard Mai let out a deep sigh and wished he could do something to help her feel, what, safe? After everything in the past day, he assumed it was just one day with all the blacking out he was doing lately, he wasn't sure anything would make them feel safe again. "Twenty seven booths, average fifteen people at each booth, and you have four hundred and five…" He trailed off as he looked at Mai, then tried to cover his mathiness with, "I'm twenty."

She quietly looked back at him and he couldn't tell if she was just about to say something or not, and feeling self conscious he pressed ahead, "I was getting all set to interview for an internship for NASA during the summer, and it was supposed to help me decide what my focus would be during my senior year because I was having a hard time deciding between computer engineering and aerospace engineering." He knew it sounded geeky, but they were being processed by unknown aliens and he realized he didn't care much. "I hadn't even turned twenty one yet." Shrugging he looked back at the floor. "I'm not sure why I'm telling you all this. I guess…"

"I just finished one year of being a teacher." Ron glanced over at Will. He remembered in the hallway Will had mentioned being a teacher, but at the time there was way too much crazy to really process that. "One year of dealing with teenagers and grading papers. I know it doesn't sound amazing, like aerospace engineering for NASA, but it was a real job, a real career. Everytime we had an official meeting I would sit there and think, wow, I'm on the inside, I've really made it. Barely twenty three years old, but I was ready for it, and now…" Will looked around meaningfully.

With that look a thought occurred to Ron, "Do you think this has anything to do with the message?"

"You know," Will continued to look around, looking like he expected something to jump out at them, "with all the running around, and kicking guards, I'd actually forgotten about that."

"Really?" Mai leaned out and looked at them both like they were lunatics. "Really?" She said it again as if she were trying to throw it at them. "Giant alien ships plow through the sky, broadcast a seriously creepy message over everyone's everything, and neither of you think this," she waved her hands around at the strange world around them, "has anything to do with it?"

"Well," Ron rolled his eyes, "when you put it like that."

Will patted Ron on the knee, "Sometimes, when the world has gone crazy, your brain has to decide what it has time to process. We were running for our lives, and fighting," he pointed at the nearest guard, "them. I don't think it's too strange to filter out things that just add to the crazy and don't help you survive in the moment."

14

Mai nodded, but looked unconvinced.

This time Ron sighed, "It was a seriously creepy message though, wasn't it?"

Mai's shoulders slumped, "Yes."

"Why do you think," Ron continued, "with all this obvious technology, they decided to patch together a bunch of old TV show footage and use that?"

Will leaned out and tilted his head trying to see into one of the cloth enclosures as the flap opened and closed to let another person in. Sitting back he said, "It was almost like a video version of a kidnapper note. You know what I mean? In those TV shows when the kidnapper would cut out letters from different magazines and paste them all together to say they have Sally and they'll only give her back for a million dollars?"

"Exactly," Ron said. "Creepy."

Mai stood up, looked at the guard, walked over and sat down on the other side of Ron. "What I think…" She paused to think for a moment. "You remember in the message how they said we were going to have to help fight whatever war this is?"

They both nodded at her.

"Well," she continued, "when they said help, I bet they meant we're going to be the cannon fodder."

Ron hadn't really given it much thought over the last few hours, but the memory of that moment wasn't something that was going to leave or fade any time soon. His first memory of it all was staring at himself in the mirror making sure his tie was straight. It was his first real job interview. He'd gotten his high school jobs because of connections with his parents, and those jobs hadn't been something you really needed to interview for. The roofing job had lasted one summer, the work topping corn was brutal the next summer because of the heat, and the worst job had been standing beside a conveyor belt as millions of cherries went past and trying to pick out the bad ones. No need to interview for cherry sorting, the bar was pretty low for that.

This job was all about math, and numbers were his favorite. He'd spent his mind numbing days beside the cherry conveyor belt averaging bad cherries per hundred as they went by. It kept him sane. A year into college and he knew what he wanted to do. He wanted to work for NASA, or anyplace that would let him figure out how to shoot a rocket into space. All that stuff required a lot of math, and it sounded great. It perfectly combined his love of space with his love of mixing and playing with numbers. Just thinking back on it brought a smile to his face. This was supposed to be a great internship that could get his foot in the door, and then the mirror rattled right off and bounced on the floor. It wasn't too surprising since it was just held onto the hollow door with some plastic hooks, but still it almost fell on his foot.

With his whole dorm shaking, all he could think was there shouldn't be any earthquakes in New Mexico. He didn't run for cover, or dash to look out the window, because nothing interesting ever happened around Albuquerque. When the shaking stopped he just shrugged and picked his phone up off the bathroom counter. Then the message came. He remembered how his phone just started talking on its own. Frozen, he found he could only stare at it. His technology had somehow betrayed him and was acting on its own. He pushed the power button and nothing happened. Flipping it over and looking at the back to see if there was a problem was when he realized he was being a little crazy. What was he hoping to see? A cord coming out the back of his phone? Someone had obviously hacked into it and all of his information was going to be lost. When he walked into the living room he realized the TV was on too. He knew his room mate hadn't left that on, and he knew he hadn't turned it on. They were saying the same thing. The idea seemed to crash through the plate glass window surrounding his brain only to lay there at his mental feet. He looked slowly at the screen on his phone then over to the TV. Not only was the sound the same, but the picture was too.

The message played on a loop at least three times, but he couldn't be sure since he'd totally ignored what was going on for the first bit. The picture and sound were made of spliced together TV and movie clips. He couldn't remember the exact message but basically it said they were there to protect us but they needed our help. There was something about a war and how they were short on manpower, or did they just say they were short on people?

"Do you remember exactly what they said?" Ron asked Mai.

She shook her head. "I didn't exactly have time to process it. It was maybe," she looked at them for confirmation of some kind, "thirty seconds to a minute at the most before everything went black and I woke up here."

Will nodded, "Now that I actually have time to think about it, and I'm not being chased down a creepy metal hallway by faceless guards, I think you're right. Once the message ended I really didn't have time to processes it before…"

"Wham," Ron smacked the back of his hand into his palm.

"Exactly."

16

Mai shushed them as a pair of guards walked over. Ron hoped it wasn't some of the guards he'd just knocked around out in the hallway. Since they still hadn't made a sound he hoped they were robots and there wouldn't be any hard feelings. Besides, you have to expect some pushback if you go around kidnapping people.

One of the guards stepped forward and pointed the rod of unconsciousness, as Ron was thinking of it, at Will and motioned for him to get up. Will looked over at the others and gave them a little smile. Ron nodded at him in a way he hoped meant something like, be strong bro, or don't worry about me, or we're all going to get through this. Any of those ideas would work. It was amazing what you could communicate through simple eye contact and a head nod.

He and Mai watched as Will was led away to the nearest booth. Ron reached over and squeezed Mai's hand. She looked at him and raised her eyebrows which he translated as, why are you grabbing my hand, I'm fine? He gave her a slight smile and sighed, she might be fine but maybe he wasn't. This was all really crazy. He just wanted someone to reassure him and let him know he wouldn't come out the other side of that booth as a cyborg with no emotions.

Mai must have understood because she squeezed his hand back and gave him a very serious nod. He wasn't sure if she was his friend, after all, they had just met, and not in the best of circumstances, but he hoped. She was pretty, and seemed smart, and nothing had fazed her yet. Hopefully, he'd be able to find her after whatever was coming next.

When the next guard motioned for him to stand up he took a deep breath and put his feet into motion. One thing he'd learned from his favorite book character, Sam Vimes, is you do the job that's in front of you. Don't worry too much about all the things going on around. You have a job and you do it. Today, this was his job. His job was to survive whatever was on the other side of that curtain.

Chapter: Mai

Mai wished she knew what tall people felt like. At five foot two and a quarter, that quarter was very important because it proved she wasn't just five foot two, she never felt like she could see what was going on around her. Sometimes it felt like the world was a place that was just happening to her instead of her being a part of it. She was always having to stand on her toes to see over, or asking people to move. The worst was when she had to get a chair to stand on. Standing in the crowd now, waiting for whatever came next, she felt like a little piece of driftwood with no control, and she really didn't like it.

She'd given Ron her brave face back in the processing center because he'd seemed lost, like he needed something. He was a bit like too many of the guys she'd known in school; solid, a little goofy, but maybe that was just because she didn't know him yet. The entire situation leading up to that hand squeeze had left her wrung out. Sitting in that hard plastic chair was like getting over the flu. Her body ached, her mind couldn't seem to catch up and stay in sync with anything, and she could feel anxiety scratching at the back of her head like a Halloween skeleton trying too hard to scare her.

When she'd finally been escorted, if you could put it as politely as that, to the next available enclosure, she thought she might puke. Will had looked so solid walking off to his possible doom, and even Ron had moved with a purpose. She stopped, took a few deep breaths and told herself they, whoever they were, wouldn't have gone to the trouble to kidnap them just to do something terrible. Looking back on that moment she wasn't sure her reasoning was sound, but it had gotten her through and that was what mattered.

She'd been able to find the guys fairly easily after she was done in the booth and together they found the line to the exit door. "So…" she looked over at them.

"Yep," Ron said, "not at all what I was expecting."

Will gave a small laugh, "And what were you expecting?"

"Not that." Ron waved back at the booths behind them.

Mai crossed her arms, "An aptitude test." She honestly was a little disgusted, "After all that. With the fighting and the anxiety, it was just an aptitude test."

"Mine," Ron turned to face both of them, "was a silver helmet that covered my face and head then started beeping." They both nodded back at him, "Then it popped off and that same voice from our rooms came on and started telling me how I did." Ron poked Mai in the shoulder as they stepped forward in the line and closer to their new future. "Well?"

"Well what?" She replied. Mai didn't really want to talk about her assessment. She needed time to process the changes from where she'd been standing before being kidnapped to what she'd just been told. It wasn't as extreme as saying her personal world had been rocked, but at the same time she wanted to say her world had been rocked.

Too many times lately she'd felt like she wasn't in control of her own life. She'd worked had to make it through college and get a business degree, but unlike Will she'd been unable to climb that ladder. In fact she'd been unable to find the ladder. So many times over the last year she thought she'd finally found something to put her energy into only to have it slip away, or given to someone else. Now, some unknown thing was trying to tell her what she was supposed to be, and she didn't know how to take it. It might be nice to have a solid direction, even if it was one that was forced on her. Part of her rebelled against that notion, but she didn't know what to do with that part. Being looked over, being looked down on, being the butt of short Asian jokes, that was what she was used to. This new thing she'd been presented with in that booth. What did she do with it?

"Don't play coy with me missy." Ron was a year younger than her, and he still seemed to have that bouncy puppyness about him sometimes, "What did the alien IQ test tell you?"

"Yeah," Will chimed in, "are you an army of one?"

"Okay, fine." Mai stopped and looked up at the ceiling and its glowing white squares of light. The voice had said a lot of things about her. Some things she totally knew already, like how she was quiet and could blend in with a crowd. That just came with the territory of being her. There were other things, however, that she wasn't sure she was ready to say out loud just yet. She wasn't sure how much she wanted to share with these two. They were nice, but she still needed processing time. Rather than tell them what actually bothered her she focused on something simple, "It seems I have steady nerves and muscle control, that's the way the voice phrased it not me."

"Oooo, you know what that means right?" Ron nudged her with his elbow.

"No, Ron, what's that mean?"

"It means you have really steady hands so you're going to be a crazy space sniper." Ron held up an invisible rifle and sighted through the attached invisible scope, "From half a quadrant away she takes out the enemy commander with a single shot."

Mai frowned and turned to Will, "And what about you?"

"It seems," Will crossed his arms and tried to look important, "my lengthy training in ancient history classes has given me a unique perspective on battle tactics."

"Oooo again, and should I add, Sir." Ron said and gave Will a quick salute.

"Don't be too impressed," Will added. "Most of my knowledge comes from people holding pointy objects and riding around on horseback. Not so much from lasers and three dimensional space warfare. However, I was told if enough people above me die I could move up the chain of command fairly quickly."

Mai shrugged she wasn't about to call him sir any time soon, "I assume that happens fairly normally in war time."

Will looked over at Ron, "What about you?"

Ron's brow furrowed as he tried to find a way to phrase what seemed to be rattling around in his head. Finally he said, "I can do really large sums of math in my head really quickly, and I have, to put it plainly, big muscles. It seems, with what they said, that they are more likely to focus on the big muscles part and not so much of the math part."

Will raised an eyebrow and Mai cocked her head to the side then said, "That's it?"

"What do you mean is that it?" Ron said.

"Well," Mai waved her hands vaguely in the air, "They told me stuff about my personality and mentioned that whole sniper thing you pointed out."

"Really?" Will and Ron said at the same time, and Mai got the feeling she needed to change the subject before they started pressing her on what else was said in her booth.

Ron continued, "They didn't say anything about my personality. What about you Will?"

"They mentioned I seemed to be able to keep calm and so would be a good candidate for a command position, but nothing more than that." Will said.

"What did they…"

Mai cut Ron off before he could continue, "Did they tell you anything about your improvements?"

"But I…" Ron tried to continue and Mai turned her back to him and walked toward the doors. She was irritated with herself for mentioning the personality stuff, and then even more irritated for using the sniper thing to cover up her mention of the personality stuff. Her assumption had been they'd all gone through the same thing in the processing, but it seemed to be tailored to each person.

Will walked past Ron, looked him in the eye, and shrugged. "They did a really fast statement at the beginning. Reminded me of car sales add where they try and fit in all the legal stuff."

Ron caught up and tried to remember all the stuff the voice said in the booth. Will was right about it being really quick. There'd been statements in there using words he didn't even understand. Aside from that, he did remember some things about standard upgrades to speed, strength, and something about a universal translator.

Will was saying something about the universal translators they all had built in now when they came to the doors. One guard watched them and another pushed the door open.

***

Ron said their little landing ship held exactly four hundred and twenty nine people, not counting the guards because He was really coming to believe they were robots. They were strapped in automatically when they sat down, and when Will asked Ron why the odd number of people, he just shrugged and pointed out empty seats.

Looking up and down the hallway of the ship Mai didn't see any indication of a flight deck, pilots, flight crew, or anything resembling intelligent beings other than the other humans on board and the guards. She knew they were on a landing ship because the voice had come on and repeated the fact many times as they climbed aboard along with the others who'd made it through the processing area with them. Eventually the message welcoming them aboard the landing ship had changed to one about getting strapped in and launching. Mai hadn't felt anything when the ship had launched except a small bump like when you hit a pothole in the road.

She ignored Ron when he tried to strike up a conversation about their new superpowers and instead tried to decide what to do next. Her big goal was to get home again. Leaving the two guys behind and trying to do it on her own crossed her mind for a fraction of a second then she decided it wasn't an option. Will really was level headed like the booth assessment had said, and Ron was, well the best way to phrase it was that he was a great sounding board. He was the kind of person who would put out the craziest theory. Did he really think it would happen? She hadn't decided on that point just yet, but it was useful.

The real reason she stayed with them was sanity. Everything had changed. The world had gone crazy, and that wasn't an exaggeration. She'd sat in that restaurant filling out another job application, which again had nothing to do with her degree, when she'd watched the world change out the window. The sky had boiled. Clouds turned deep red and the thing moving through them look like a flaming branch swung by a kid around a campfire. It left a trail of smoke and ruin as it moved over the countryside. From Mai's perspective it seemed to move at a turtle's pace, but she knew it was all disjointed perspective. The thing was massive. The shadow it cast blotted out the entire landscape, covering trees and fields for miles and causing all the lights to come on in town.

Then came the message with it's almost hilariously disjointed broadcast telling them they were all being conscripted into some larger war. Not only had aliens finally shown up, but when they did they brought with them all their problems. Like so many others, she'd seen her share of science fiction shows. Most of them were action packed with explosions and cute girls unnecessarily running around in tank tops. In reality, she'd hoped, if aliens were out there, they'd make things better. Technology to feed the hungry, cure disease, and help us colonize other worlds. Part of the mental shift was finding out that aliens weren't like either of those things. They didn't come to conquer the world by blowing up all the national landmarks, and they didn't bring peace and prosperity. Instead they showed up with bad audio and visual files and kidnapped her.

The two guys sitting on either side of her helped remind her of reality and kept her focused. They were like a filter for the crazy. Alone, she would've had to deal with all of it at once, and she wasn't sure she could've done that. With the guys there she could let them deal with some of it while she got to pick and choose what crazy she let in. Unfortunately there seemed to be some things she didn't really have a choice about. Like the improvements. She'd tried her best over the last few hours to catch a glimpse of her reflection, so far she didn't see anything different, but she knew they were there. Mai had freaked out, like any sane person should in her situation, and ran from the first guards she'd seen when she'd come out of her room. Surprising herself she outran them easily, and she never ran anywhere. At first she just chalked it up to adrenaline, but then she broke things. The first console she and Ron had come to. She told herself it was a coincidence, or it was going to break anyway, but then there were other things. She left fingerprints in door frames. She'd broken one of the metal poles holding up her testing booth.

Speaking of her testing, that was another thing she didn't really want to think about. Some alien going into her mind and telling her… Anyway, she didn't really agree with it, and she definitely didn't have to do anything they told her. If Ron thought it only meant she could be some space sniper then that was where she was going to leave it.

Feeling a slight bump she heard the voice say, "Welcome to the largest moon of the Percian system. The gravity here is less than that on Earth so watch your step. The atmosphere inside the bubble is habitable so please don't leave the confines of the habitat. Once you have disembarked you will be outfitted and assigned to your new unit."

The harnesses disengaged, the door opened, and she got her first real look at another world. The ground she stepped down onto was gray and dust kicked up when she landed on it. Her brain immediately jumped to images of Neil Armstrong's boot print on the moon. Above her loomed a planetary orb covered in red and yellow clouds. No sign of land or water, just clouds covering everything. The air tasted stale with a slight metallic tinge to it, as if she'd just bitten her tongue.

"I wonder why they didn't just transport us down?" Ron said from behind her.

"Huh," Will stopped and looked around, "I don't know."

"Probably just the time constraints of the whole thing. They didn't want to take the time, or they didn't have the time, when they kidnapped us all, or maybe they don't want to use the teleporter since people aren't all getting through those booths at the same time." Ron was looking up at the hovering ball of the planet above them. "Looks like a super bouncy ball I used to have."

"Maybe it's too expensive." Mai tossed the idea out there, not because she thought it was the reason but because she wanted to talk about something other than what to do now.

"Nah," Ron said, "I doubt money has anything to do with it, but maybe too expensive in terms of power costs. You'd need a lot of computing power to zap all of us around at the same time. Each molecule in the human body needs to be mapped and positioned in space and time so that when you move it and resemble it you can put everything back in the right order. With the moon moving at one speed and the ship moving at a different speed along with the fact that time moves differently the closer you get to the gravity well of the planet…"

Mai watched as Ron started ticking imaginary numbers in the air with his fingers.

"Or," Will chimed in, "they didn't want to scramble us."

Mai had a mental image of dropping an egg, "They didn't seem to care about doing that on the way to the ship."

"True, but at that point they could break a few eggs," she wondered if he'd read her mind somehow, "and not really care because they had so many others that statistically it wouldn't matter."

"But now…" She added for him.

"But now, they've put time and equipment into improving us." Mai could hear the air quotes Will vocally put around the word improve. "Now we're valuable eggs."

"That's a lot of quantum computers." Ron said to the sky.

"What?" Mai looked over at him.

He looked over at her, "In order to move that many molecules not only would you need tons of quantum computers but a couple of stars worth of energy to run them."

"So?"

"So, I just don't get how they could have the technology to do all that and still need us to fight a war for them," Ron said. "Why not just build robots at that point?"

"And why," Will added, "can't they do a better job of making a message for the whole world to hear?"

Four guards had been slowly moving the newly arrived crowd toward what looked like a pair of train freight cars. Light spilled out of the nearest end and Mai, once again, decided this was some crazy she could let the others handle. She looked over at Will, waggled her fingers at their destination and asked, "What do you think?"

"They said," he leaned closer to Mai and Ron, "we are supposed to get outfitted. By they I mean the creepy voice. I assume get outfitted means to get new gear."

Ron grinned, "They could be giving us cool space guns, or jet packs, or…" he trailed off as his brain overloaded on the possibilities of the alien technology he was about to receive.

Ron and Mai lined up at one and Will was pushed toward the other. Will was waiting for her at the other end and as Mai stepped out she finally understood Ron's mentality. She truly and completely felt like a badass for the first time in her life. They had, to her total surprise, not only lived up to Ron's dream about space guns and jet packs but surpassed it in ways she wasn't even sure of.

Ron didn't just come out of the outfitting center, he leaped and landed in his most heroic pose possible, "The video said we can't use them inside the bubble," he shifted to another heroic pose, "but I totally want to figure out what a supersonic flechette is. Also, what did it mean when it said there was a sub cranial nano biotic interface?"

Mai laughed. She couldn't help it. All the stress of the last twenty four hours, all the worries and fears, the mental trauma of having her life ripped away from her, vanished for that one moment. Part of her wanted to say this was no time for laughter, but she ignored it. Ron stood there perfectly highlighted by an alien planet looking for all the world like the cover of a video game.

Their suits were all made of similar material, but were obviously different. They all had, what looked like, interchangeable parts such as the solid armor pieces. She was fairly sure they were the same things the guards had been wearing on the spaceship, just ramped up a few notches. Her suit had fewer of the solid plates which allowed her a much greater range of movement than Ron, who basically looked like a walking tank. That wasn't to say he seemed to be restricted in any way. In fact, the more she looked at it the more certain she was that his suit actually changed when he moved. The solid pieces seemed to slide and reform to accommodate whatever he was doing.

Ron's suit was mainly white but had blue outlines along with blue gloves and boots. Mai, looking down at herself, noted her much more dampened color scheme. Her armor plates were still white, but they were a dull white, not the polished white of Ron's. Her trim was gray and looking down at herself she noted that her boots blended into the moon dust perfectly. Will, taller than either of them, looked every bit the commander his profile back on the ship said he should be. His armor was somewhere in-between Mai's and Ron's when it came to sheer bulk, but had what looked like an extra screen attached to the backside of his left forearm. His suit was the standard white, the same as Ron's, but his trim was red.

"It's like medieval armor." Will said as he walked over to them. He bounced up and when he landed he flexed his legs down into a squat then back up, "Except it doesn't pinch you every time you move." She watched as he leaned over and rapped his knuckles on his shins, "I don't know what this stuff is but it's cool."

The armor covered every major part with only the joints being flexible material instead of the solid white. The boots were embarrassingly comfortable, and, after running her fingers over a large rock next to them, realized that somehow she could feel everything she touched through the gloves. It was almost like they weren't even there.

"I really don't want to think about what they had to do to my brain to get that to work." Ron had squatted down and was poking a rock over and over.

"What do you mean?" Mai asked.

"I can feel the edge of the rock, and I'm wearing really big gloves. That means," he picked up the rock and looked at it, "they had to get the input from the gloves to interface with my nervous system," he paused and looked at her, "in my brain Mai. They put stuff in my brain. I mean, am I even me anymore? Am I just a robot copy of me? Did they take my DNA and build a clone of me and this is now me, but the real me is on a slab somewhere in cold storage back in their ship?"

Will stepped up, "I know this is going to sound really heartless right now because Ron, while crazy, has a really good point, but we need to focus on more important matters."

"More important than..." Ron pointed his right hand at a larger rock and flexed his fist. A small compartment popped up from the back of his arm and small puffing noises came out. At the same time a chunk of the rock broke off accompanied by a metallic ringing sound. Around them Mai heard someone scream and turned to see a woman more than fifty feet away clutching at a metal spike embedded in the thigh of her new armor.

"Whoa, whoa, there killer." Will grabbed Ron's arm and pushed it down.

The compartment sunk back into his arm while a look of shock and wonder leaped onto Ron's face followed by embarrassment. "Sorry," he waved with his free hand at the woman who was now sitting on the ground trying to pull the spike out. "Well, I guess now we know what a flechette is."

"And yes, Ron," Will let go of his arm, "there are some things more important that you fooling around with your new alien battle suit."

"That's not what I meant to do. I mean, it is, but it's not the point I was trying to get across." Ron looked from Mai to Will and back, "I didn't pull a trigger. I didn't say any commands. I just thought it, and it happened. I know I've kinda set myself up as the space nerd here, but that," he pointed to the spot on his forearm where the flechettes had popped out, "freaks me out."

"Yes," Will said, "I totally agree that having stuff," he waved at his head, "is not what I really wanted to happen to me, but right now the important thing is to find a way to get home."

"Now that we have all of this," Mai knocked on Ron's chest plate, "it should be a lot easier."

"Maybe not," Will replied.

"Why not?" Ron raised both his hands and clenched his fists. Mai flinched expecting some new form of death to pop out of his suit somewhere.

Will reached out and again lowered Ron's arms, "Because, with technology like this I expect they can keep track of us and are monitoring our conversations right now."

Ron looked chagrined and nodded, "True, true. However, we could…" He reached up and tapped his chin.

Mai flinched again.

"Seriously?" Ron looked her in the eyes and held it for a beat before saying, "You have to think about what you want to happen, and order the suit to do it. Something's not going to shoot out when I have my hand pointed at my own face."

Mai took a deep breath and realized Ron was right. She needed to calm down. "You're right. Now, what were you thinking of?"

"Will might be right about the tracking and listening stuff, but there's really only one way to find out."

Will looked around to see if they were alone. As they'd been talking more people had arrived and added their presence to the thousands already standing around on the moon. They definitely weren't alone. On the other hand, Mai thought, there is a certain truth about being alone in a crowd. With so much going on, and so many people getting outfitted in new gear, no one was really paying much attention to them.

Will looked at Mai and Ron and said clearly, "I am going to test out my new weapons by blowing up that outfitting center I just came through. In fact," Will raised his voice, "I'm so angry about being kidnapped and taken from my family that I'm going to just go nuts and start shooting anything and blowing stuff up at random."

They all stood there and waited. Nothing happened. Mai looked around for one of the guards to see if they were headed their way. She saw two of them and they were just leaning against the outside of another outfitting post.

"You know," she said, "Ron did shoot someone in the leg and no one did anything about it."

"This is true," Ron said, "I did. In my defense, it is the first person I've ever shot, and I really didn't know what I was doing. Also," he leaned out a bit and looked for the woman he'd shot, "she does seem to be just fine."

"All right," Will said, "If they are listening they don't seem to care about us."

"Maybe," Mai added, "They only care about us as a mass of humanity and don't really care about individuals."

Will nodded, "Either way, I say we take advantage of this situation and try to find a way out of here."

"Attention please!" The voice they'd all come to recognize blared out, "Will all guards please begin moving the outfitted persons toward the disembarkation center now."

This message repeated three times then stopped. Mai looked over to where she'd seen the two guards lounging around and saw they were now pushing through the masses of humanity and pointing people to an unseen destination off to her right.

"If we're going to do something…" She was cut off by the arrival of another person.

"Excuse me, but I couldn't help but hear that y'all were planning an escape?"

The newcomer was almost the same height as Will but with short cut blonde hair and freckles across his nose. Mai placed him as late teens early twenties, but other than that it was hard to tell much about him with the standard armor covering up everything else. His armor was the white with blue trim, like Ron's. Because of this she realized the colors must designate something. Most likely not rank since none of them had enough time to earn any of that, but maybe it said what your job was. Red was officer corps, because she figured that's what Will would end up as. Blue must be infantry, or something like that. Not because she thought Ron was dumb, just because he seemed like he would have more fun standing in the front holding a really big gun. Her gray was, well, she wasn't quite sure, and didn't really want to think over her mental profile again.

"Yes," Will said quietly while glancing around to see how close the guards were, "Why? Do you want to come with us? Do you have something helpful?"

Mai was a bit shocked that Will was instantly going to trust this guy. They didn't know him. He could be... She stopped herself and realized she was about to think the dumbest thing. He could be what? A spy? Working for the aliens? A few hours ago she didn't know who Will or Ron were and she trusted them with her life now. Why? Because they were all human, and in this situation it was all that mattered. This guy was human, and he wanted to go home just like they did.

"Yes to all of that." He said. Mai liked his drawl and decided to call him Tex, but only in her head. She didn't want to get on the wrong side of someone when they were standing on a moon orbiting an unknown planet.

"I was wondering around," he gestured back toward the landing shuttles, "and on a side note, have any of you noticed how little these guys seem to care if you just wander around?"

"I know," Ron said, "I shot someone and they didn't do anything."

"Really?" Tex looked over at Ron.

"It was an accident." Will added.

"Anyway," Tex continued, "I was wandering off that way after I got my spacesuit and I saw a bunch of those guards pushing..." he paused and looked around for a good word, "floating boxes through a thing..."

"Through a thing?" Mai said. "Could you be more specific?"

"Well, the thing is," Tex said, "I can't really be more specific because it's kinda insane and I'm still not sure how to describe it. It was a pillar of stone about the height of a basketball hoop, and there were these guys, they were dressed like the guards," he looked around at them to see if they knew what he meant, "they were pushing these floating boxes right toward the pillar and they just..." He paused and shrugged like the explanation should just come floating out of the air by itself.

"They just what?" Will encouraged him to continue.

"Well the air..." he paused again. "The thing is..." He sighed heavily. "They disappeared." He raised his hands to ward off what he expected to be an onrush of accusations.

Ron nodded, and Will realized this wasn't even close to the craziest thing they had been through in the last few hours. Boxes disappeared when run into some stone monolith. No big deal, but how could they use this to their advantage?

Will nodded encouragingly, "So why do you think they were pushing these boxes into the..." He wasn't sure what to call it, "The thing that made them disappear?"

Tex shrugged, "How should I know?"

"Then why is it important?" Mai asked.

"Oh, right." Tex nodded. "The thing..."

"Monolith," Ron interrupted. They all looked at him and he shrugged. "The thing was a big stone sticking up out of the ground, right?"

Tex nodded.

"Did it look like natural stone or was it all polished up and man, or in this case alien, made looking?"

"Well," Tex thought about it, "it looked natural, but it also looked like it had been cut out of a larger chunk of something."

"Okay," Ron nodded as if this explained everything, "a monolith."

Will sighed. Annoyingly, Mai realized Ron was right. Any American watching a normal amount of television would know at least a little about the standing stones all over Europe, especially the British Isles, called monoliths. She knew a little about Stonehenge, but her favorite standing stones would have to be the ones from the movie Brave.

"All right, the monolith, as you called it, messed up how everything around it looked and when they pushed the boxes toward it they would disappear. So I assumed..." He left it hanging and shrugged.

Ron nodded and said, "It's cargo, supplies of some kind. Us people", he waved a hand at the mass of humanity being herded by the guards, "are most likely going somewhere to get a little bit more training and be divided up into platoons and such. The supplies are going somewhere else."

"Good thinking." Will said. "Now we just need something that looks like a clipboard and a box to push."

"What?" Mai looked at Ron to see if he'd understood what Will had just said. Ron shrugged and looked back over at Will.

"It's something you learn if you ever work inside a bureaucracy of any kind, especially the military." Will said, "As long as you look like you know where you're going, and you have a list of some kind to check off, no one will bother you."

Chapter: Will

As they crossed through, the shiver Will felt reminded him of stepping from the air conditioning at the mall into a one hundred and four degree parking lot. It always felt like someone was grabbing his scalp and pulling it back like a skin ponytail.

The monolith had looked more or less like Tex had described it. It was around ten feet tall and cut from some kind of rough gray stone. It wasn't exactly straight but jagged like an old man's tooth sticking up from the lunar dust. As they'd approached it he realized exactly what Tex had meant by things getting messed up around it. The closer they came the more it seemed like they were looking through the curved glass of a fish bowl. However, stepping through it was almost like stepping through a door. They didn't stumble or lurch. He took a step on a moon and that step ended on a dirt path here in another world. He didn't want to dwell on what stepping through that gash in reality was doing to his body. Words like radiation poisoning sprung to mind, but he had more immediate issues to deal with, and hopefully his new alien space suit would protect him from things like that.

Through the visor on his helmet he could see a new world. Gone was the gray monotone of whatever moon they'd been on, and before him was a green verdant world. There was a trail leading from the ring they'd all just stepped through, and on each side trees spread out as far as he could see. At least he temporarily classified them as trees. They had a brown trunk that reminded him of pines, but the branches and pine needles had been replaced by single large flat leaves. Each one attached to the trunk then spread out to larger than six feet across. Beneath them grass and bushes swayed in the breeze. Some were red others green, and they grew to about three feet in height causing the forest around him to seem all but impenetrable.

He was surprised, and delighted, to notice that his visor didn't seem to block any colors and also acted like sunglasses. The smell of the place reminded him of going camping with his family, but not just that, it was the smell right after a rain. It was fresh and… He paused and realized he could smell it and his helmet was still securely fastened, or at least he hoped it was. At this thought a message appeared on his visor, "Helmet and suit integrity at 100%. Atmosphere is 95% breathable. Helmet removal is within acceptable limits."

Nice, he thought, I'm really starting to like this suit, even if it does creep me out. Now that he knew the air wouldn't kill him he decided to stick with plan A anyway and keep the helmet on and the visor down. They'd decided, back on the moon, that there would be less possible questions if they just looked like soldiers and not like humans. Tearing his eyes away from the stunning view, and suppressing questions about how his suit interacted with his thoughts, he noticed an offshoot of the trail to the right leading to where he could just see in the distance a tent was surrounded by similar looking boxes and a few vehicles.

Will turned to the others, "All right," they'd practiced with the suits before coming through and had figured out how to create a radio link between themselves and hopefully leave everyone else out. "Just like we talked about."

The four of them pushed their stolen boxes toward the supply dump and as they got close enough two figures emerged from the tent. The first was human shaped and wearing armor with green trim around the white, but its helmet was off and caused Will to stopped walking for a moment. It wasn't every day you come into contact with a real alien, and while they had been in a spaceship and walked around on a moon they hadn't actually seen a real live alien. His skin was powder blue with darker spots that, Will assumed, were like freckles. In place of hair there was a red ridge running from his forehead down the back of his neck, which reminded Will of granite sticking up out of the soft soil on a mountain top.

"Now that," Ron's voice paused while the second alien emerged from the tent, "is creeping me out."

"It's…" Will trailed off.

"It's a centaur spider, thing," Ron said.

"Naw, it can't be a spider." Tex added then nudged them to start walking again.

"What?" Mai said.

"It can't be a spider thing," Tex repeated. "It's only got six legs."

Will noticed Tex was right. The thing, or alien, coming toward them had a human torso covered in armor with the same green trim, but the bottom half was a horizontal body of some kind with six segmented legs. The movement of the legs was almost hypnotic and Will tried to stop himself from staring before remembering he couldn't be seen through his darkened visor.

The not a spider centaur alien put out a hand and motioned for them to stop, "And what are you four doing here."

Will knew he was just hearing a translation from whatever language this thing spoke, but even so, he could hear the irritation in its voice. The best way to deal with all of this, Will had explained to the others before they came through, was to say you were just following orders.

"We were told to come here and help move things up." and to be vague, Will thought. It's easier to lie if you don't include too many details.

"And what's in the box?" Spider centaur alien gestured at the four boxes they'd been pushing a moment before.

"Spentaur?" Ron's whisper buzzed through Will's helmet, and though part of him wanted to smile at the attempt most of him wanted to smack Ron in the head.

"How should I know?" Will replied to the alien. "We were pulled aside, told to go though there," He pointed with his thumb over his shoulder at the ring they'd just come through, "and help move things up."

"See," the spentaur, now Will could only think of it like that thanks to Ron, turned to the blue skinned guy, "I told you this was all going to be a marsh with no bridge."

Will assumed his translator hadn't handled the idiom well and decided his best course of action was to simply wait for them to make the next move.

The blue alien grunted, pointed his finger at the first box, and they all watched as words appeared on top. From what Will could tell, just glancing at it, the box seemed to be full of food rations of some kind. He had no idea what a centaur thing might eat.

"Look," the blue one turned back to the centaur, "you need to lighten up. If they were told to move some of this up to the front, then who are we to…"

"Who are we?" The centaur interrupted him, "We are the ones in charge of the supplies for this entire battalion. We are the ones who are going to be called upon to justify why things either are where they're supposed to be or aren't where they're supposed to be. These," he waved his arm at the boxes, "aren't on my list, and you may be fine with shirking protocol but I'm not."

Mai stepped around Will and looked up at the centaur's face which was easily two feet higher than her own, "Look," she took another step forward forcing the centaur to back up so he could keep eye contact with her, "we have a limited amount of time to do our job, if you get my meaning."

"Well I don't…"

The blue guy grabbed the centaur's arm to stop him from talking, "Now, see here, Gray, we don't want any trouble. We didn't see you back there."

The centaur leaned forward, "Gray, you say?"

"Don't mind him," Blue interrupted again, "Those eyes of his don't always catch certain colors, and that one does seem to blend in." The emphasis he placed on the word Gray practically dripped off his tongue.

"Well," the centaur pulled up a screen on its arm, "we were planning on packing the eight wheeler and taking supplies up later today…"

"Exactly," blue said, "and if you all wanted to do that for us, then we should be thanking you for letting us have the afternoon off."

Mai's exasperated grunt could be heard through her helmet, "Good."

Will stepped forward, "All right, let's get the eight wheeler loaded and move out."

Because of the antigravity technology it was quick work to load up the vehicle which was very appropriately named the eight wheeler. It was flat with magnetic locks for the boxes and one spot up front for a driver. During the loading process Will glanced over at Mai but didn't want to ask her what had just happened, because it might blow their cover.

Once they were loaded Tex jumped into the driver's seat, put his hand against what looked like a screen, and the eight wheeler rumbled into action. In reality there wasn't much rumbling. The thing was whisper quiet except for the crunch of the ground under all those tires.

Ron jumped on top of one of the boxes and sat next to Mai, "That was kick ass."

"What?" she said.

"Aww, don't give me that." Ron nudged her with his elbow, "You just faced down the creepiest thing I've ever seen, and you did it like a boss."

Will walked behind the eight wheeler, which wasn't difficult since the thing defined the term plodding. Once they were out of sight, which wasn't too hard with all the trees, he popped his helmet open and took a deep breath of the open air. "I feel like I've been locked inside a metal box for the last few days."

"I guess, in a way, we have." Mai said and opened the visor on her helmet.

For a moment Will was able to pretend he was back home. The smell of the dirt road and the forest around them was perfect. Memories of walking through slightly damp forests around Portland and Seattle carried his mind away like a stick on a river. He could hear someone humming from father up and assumed it was Tex, and without realizing it they'd covered miles. He wasn't sure how he knew but when he looked around and specifically wondered how far they'd gone something in his brain popped up with an answer. All of these enhancements were starting to worry him. What exactly had they put in his head? Apparently he was still able to lie since here he was with boxes of stolen goods, and either they couldn't track him or they just didn't care yet.

The humming sound changed, and the pitch of it caused a picture with explanation of a rocket to pop into his mind. Just as he was wondering what that was all about the ground in front of him exploded and he was shoved backward by an invisible punch to the chest. His visor snapped shut and the eight wheeler was outlined in blue as it dropped toward him. For a moment he wondered if he was improved enough to catch it but decided rolling out of the way was the better course of action. Pushing himself to his feet he took cover behind the now crash landed eight wheeler and looked around for any other survivors.

Ron was crouched off to the right behind a tumble of boxes, and when he wondered where Mai was, a blinking gray diamond on his visor told him she was back in the woods behind him somewhere. The attack came from the tree line opposite their position with the initial shots sounding more like a chainsaw than the pop pop Will had expected from gunfire.

Poking his head over the edge of the tipped eight wheeler his suit identified five sources of gunfire, and immediately he was worried about being flanked on both sides. With just the two of them holding this position Will knew it would be all too easy for them to get pinned down while the soldiers on the edges swung around their meager protection to tear them up with ease.

"Ron?" He almost whispered.

"I hear ya, chief."

His simple reply brought Will's blood pressure down an octave. He'd assumed they'd be able to communicate but wasn't sure if there was anything special he needed to do. "Take out the guy on your far right, and I'll go after the one on the left." He paused and hoped, "Mai?" There was no response. "Mai." He wanted to put more emphasis onto it, but didn't want to yell.

"I'm here." The irritation in her voice brought out a powerpoint presentation of memories for him. All the slides were of annoying students who just needed to do what they were told. His teeth ached and he realized he was clenching his jaw. Why was she pushing back at a time like this. He took a deep breath and said, "Anybody pokes their head out of the trees while Ron and I are shooting at people..."

"I know what I'm doing, Will."

"See," Ron said, brushing aside the growing tension, "badass sniper."

"Shut up Ron." Mai whispered, and Will could almost hear Ron grin.

Chapter: Ron

He'd caught Mai's tone of voice. It might be better to say they'd all been bashed over the head with the tree trunk of Mai's tone of voice, but he'd decided playing it off was the best way to go. Nothing could be gained by arguing while being shot at, and Ron figured if he kept at it she might actually smile at him.

Ron didn't wait for Will to say go. When people are actively trying to kill you sometimes sitting around isn't the best idea. He dug his fancy new space war suit boots into the soft dirt and pushed hard, launching himself to the right and straight at a large tree like thing. Putting his hand and foot out he used the tree to change his trajectory and shot across the road as quickly as he could. His suit visor told him the soldier farthest to the right of the encounter was now directly in front of him, it also told him he'd been shot a few times. He hadn't felt anything so he decided to worry about that later. Back on earth he wasn't even old enough to have a stiff drink of something to help him with his courage. Age, and his lost chance at that NASA internship didn't really seem to matter, right now his main concern was which of the many weapons available to him should he use first, and where the shooter was standing.

Formulas for tracing bullet trajectory unraveled through his mind. A triangle floated in his mind with one point being the gun barrel another point being the ground and the third point being him. He could get the speed of the projectile from his suit sensors, he assumed, and as soon as he assumed it data appeared on his visor telling him the type and speed of the round he'd been hit by. With the short distance traveled and the massive speed of the bullet he knew there wouldn't been much arc to the shot. However, he ran into a mental problem when he realized he didn't know the gravity of this particular planetary body and he also didn't know the density of the atmosphere the bullet was traveling through. Fortunately he could just brute force the equation because, again, they were shooting at him from a relatively close range and doing it repeatedly. This gave him enough real world data that the abstract parts didn't really matter. So, ignoring the gravity of the situation, he chuckled at his his own mental pun, he got down to deciding on what instrument of death and destruction he should reply with.

There was a flamethrower, but with all the wet vegetation around that didn't seem useful. The flechette thing could be good. It wouldn't be stopped by leaves and branches. He raised his arm while dodging around a tree and his visor told him where to point. In a way it felt like so many video games. Get the crosshairs over the silhouette of the bad guy and shoot. Granted, he was sure that was also what the bad guy was doing, so moving and shooting were very important.

From off to his left he heard something explode and decided Will might have a good idea. His little metal spikes weren't really doing much, at least nothing he could see, so something bigger was needed. A list of possibilities went through his mind and he was reminded again of how creepy it was to have all this stuff in his head. He settled on a cluster of sticky bombs and waited to get a good shot of his opponent. Once the red ring of death had settled into place over the bad guy, he mentally pulled the trigger. Something the size of a baseball popped out of his right shoulder and turned into a bright red indicator on his visor. A warning blinked at him telling him he was too close, and not wanting to be blown up by his own bombs he changed direction. A few jumps brought him back to the road just as a very large explosion caused chunks of trees, dirt, and other unknown things to drop around him like evil rain.

His suit warned him two other bad guys were coming up on his right fast. Turning and intentionally falling backward he extended his left hand and let out a shotgun blast of tiny metal needles from the compartment in his forearm. The soldier closest to him staggered backward, his visor full of cracks and holes. As he landed on his back, he watched the next soldier raise a very large object which his improved brain told him could only be the gun making the chainsaw noises earlier, but rather than raining down a tsunami of bullets Ron saw him lurch sideways and collapse to the roadway.

Mai's voice tickled his ear, "You're welcome."

Raising himself up on his elbows he scanned the area. His visor didn't show anymore bad guys, but he really didn't know how it identified them in the first place. Maybe if they stood still and didn't shoot at him they wouldn't show up. "Will?"

"I'm here."

"You see anymore of them?"

"No," Will paused, "at least not that I can tell." Ron could hear a question mark in Will's voice, and realized he was thinking the same thing he'd wondered. "Mai," As Ron stood up he could see Will walking toward him, "do you see any more bad guys?"

"Nope."

"Right," Ron watched Will turn a slow circle, "let's meet back at the eight wheeler."

Ron's suit chimed at him while he was walking toward the scattered boxes and tipped over vehicle. The display on his visor showed a layout of his suit with spots marked in red with blinking exclamation marks over them. When he looked at it the display zoomed in and gave a quick readout of the damage to that area followed by a message in yellow, "Raw Materials Needed".

"And what does that mean?"

"What?" Mai stepped out of the tree line and Ron started to raise his arm, a gun extending from his forearm. "Whoa there," she raised her hands toward him.

"Don't do that." He said, the gun sinking back into his suit like a submarine diving below the surface.

"Do what? Walk out of the trees in an open and obvious way?"

"After being shot at from those very same trees, I'm going to say yes, don't do that." Ron replied.

"Anyway," she said and he could tell she was rolling her eyes even with her visor down, "who were you talking to?"

"Who was I…" confused for a moment he had to think back and was reminded by the blinking red and yellow images on his display. "Oh, right. My visor is telling me I need raw materials."

Will was waiting for them at the tipped over eight wheeler and chimed in, "Mine is too."

"Well mine," Mai added, "seems to be fine." She stopped on the other side of Ron, very clearly wanting to keep him between her and Will.

"And that's because you weren't getting shot at by an evil space version of a machine gun." Ron brought his hand up and formed a gun with his fingers, "pew, pew, pew." He really didn't do well with conflict, and his fall back position in this fight was to use humor. Sometimes bad humor. Realistically, it was usually bad humor, but that was just because it's hard to actually be funny when you're uncomfortable, and this was uncomfortable.

The three of them hardly knew each other, and they had been thrust together in the craziest situation. Ron had instantly taken a liking to Mai back on the mothership, and when they'd run, literally in this case, into Will he'd thought things were great. Turns out sometimes his judgement of such things wasn't as good as his grasp of calculous. Thinking back on what had just happened he still wasn't sure why Mai had tossed attitude at Will like a bad tennis ball. Wait, he looked back at forth between Mai and Will. A tennis ball? Who says things like that? That was a bad metaphor even for him. Come to think of it he was fairly sure it was actually a simile. His mind was spinning, trying to find the definition for the difference between a metaphor and a simile while actually just waiting for the uncomfortable silence to end.

An audible deep breath came over the line from Will's suit and Ron wondered why they all still had their visors down. Will stepped forward so he could face Mai but still gave a good bit of personal space. His visor flipped up as he said, "Do you have a problem with me?"

Ron wanted to answer and turn it all into a joke, but he knew it wouldn't help. Mai's visor lifted and she met Will's gaze, "I barely know you. How could I have a problem with you?"

"And yet…" He waved his hand and Ron was amazing at how something as simple as that could indicate the entire interaction that had happened before the firefight.

"It's just that," she paused, her lips pressing together holding back the words, "people in charge lately have…" She stopped again. "No. I don't have a problem with you. I have a problem with this whole situation, and all of," she waved her hands at the armor she was wearing. "On top of it, I just killed a guy, and I really don't know how to handle it."

Will stood there quietly for a moment, nodded to her, looked over at Ron, and said, "Actually, It was more like, chuga, chuga, chuga, just faster."

Ron grinned and nodded at the break in the tension, then realized no one could see it with his visor down, and with a thought flipped it up, "Exactly." He reached down and picked up a branch that had been blown off one of the trees around them during the initial explosion. Aiming it at the road he started to make the same sound but sped up when the branch turned to dust. "What the…"

Stepping back from it, Ron looked from the dust drifting to the ground to his companions, "Did you see that?"

Will walked over and picked up a second branch and held it out in front of himself. A moment later it too dissolved into dust.

"So, dead trees on this planet disintegrate?" Ron looked around at the surrounding trees wondering what a whole dead tree would do.

"Nope," Will replied, "when it disappeared my display said raw materials had been acquired and one red area turned yellow. It now says that it is in progress, but the other areas still need raw material."

Mai was looking intently at another branch, "The suits are using the cellular structure of the wood as raw material to repair the damage."

"And since you didn't take any damage…" Will responded.

"I don't need any repairs." She finished.

"So," Ron flipped his visor back down, "I wonder if a rock would work or if just the branches…" He picked up a rock the size of a pumpkin and watched as it slowly dissolved from his hands. "That is wild. I wonder what would happen if I touched a person? Are there safeguards in place? Would it check to see if the person was alive or dead?"

"Speaking of…" Mai's voice sounded strange and Ron wasn't too sure about strange right now. Three different guns popped out when he turned toward her. They slowly retracted when he saw what she was looking at.

A pair of boots lay on the ground. One looked like the remains of a birthday candle left to burn for too long. The material oozed down revealing the top of what was left of a foot. "Tex." Will said.

Ron felt the contents of his stomach twitch upward and clenched his teeth. His mind latched onto the first thought to flit through his brain, would the suit use his vomit as raw materials to repair itself? Looking away to keep himself from finding the answer to his question, he wondered aloud, "What now?"

"Well," Will started to answer him. Ron could hear someone digging and realized, even though he'd barely known him, Tex had been a human, and in this of all situations he deserved some kind of burial. "I think," Will continued, "we have two basic options, and you two can agree or disagree as you like since I'm not really your commanding officer."

Ron turned to see Mai dusting off her hands over the top of a new mound of dirt. She crossed herself, "I have no idea where you came from Tex or what kind of person you were, but here, so far from home, I really do pray your soul finds its way to someone or something that loves you."

"Amen," Ron and Will echoed each other, and for a quiet moment it didn't matter that they were lost somewhere in space.

"So," Mai broke the silence, "what were those two options you were talking about?"

"Right," Will nodded, "but first..." he turned and grabbed a box fallen from the eight wheeler and set it flat. Placing two more of them he gestured for them to sit. "I figured we could use a place to sit if we're going to have a real meeting." They sat and when Will flipped his visor up the other two followed suit. "We're trying to get across an unknown amount of space, and I see two means of doing that. First, we can commandeer some kind of a ship and try to fly it home, but I see some problems with that."

Mai nodded, "Like the fact that none of us would know how to fly it."

"Our suits might," Ron added.

"True," Will said, "I hadn't thought of that."

"But," Mai cut back in, "Our suits might not let us steal a ship from the people who made them, and the only way to know is to find out the hard way."

Ron nodded as they all sat for a moment thinking then added, "Also, we don't know which way to go."

"That's part of the first problem," Mai said. "If we could figure out how to fly the ship then, most likely, the ship itself would have some kind of star chart or autopilot."

"Especially since they did just kidnap about a billion of us from Earth." Will said.

"Yeah, you'd think that would be marked on a map." Ron agreed.

Will nodded, "So, the main problem with that plan is back to the fact none of us know how to fly the ship, and even if our suits do, we aren't sure if they will."

"Actually," Mai raised her hand like a kid in class.

"Yes," Will nodded at her.

"The main problem with that plan is a bit more obvious." She slowly gestured at the surrounding countryside, "No ship."

"And that leads us to option number two," Will said.

Ron sighed, "And that is?"

"The monoliths."

"The what?" Mai said looking from Ron to Will.

"You know," Ron replied. "The big magic rock we walked directly into and wound up on a different planet."

"Ahhh..." Mai nodded. "There have been so many things that I lose track when something isn't directly shooting at me."

"I figure we find the next monolith and head through it..." Will waved his hand in the air with a rolling motion.

42

"And we just keep going through them until we either get home or find a ship we can borrow." Mai finished.

"That is a terrible plan." Ron said. "The monoliths will be guarded, or on enemy territory, or on the other side of the planet, or…"

Mai raised her hand to cut him off, "True, and true, but what other option do we have. There's nothing here for us to use, so…"

Will nodded, "So we keep moving until we find something we can use. Plus, so far, no one has seemed too concerned about three recruits moving around unsupervised."

Ron rolled his eyes, "And how long is that going to last if we start jumping through guarded monoliths? Our little trick this morning isn't going to work every time."

Mai raised her hand again, but this time added some shushing sounds to it. Her visor dropped and she looked around. Ron immediately did the same and saw, coming down the road, figures outlined in blue on his display. He wondered if blue was supposed to mean good guys when his display added the tag "Friendly" above the heads of the oncoming soldiers. "Great," throwing his hands in the air he wondered if his suit would let him shoot at the friendly targets, "now what?"

"We tell the truth." Will said.

"What?" Ron looked over at him.

"We got attacked while we were trying to deliver these supplies." Will stood up. "the worst that can happen is they take us to whatever base camp exists and we have to figure a way out of there."

Mai looked around at the jumbled crates, "I wonder if there was a map in any of these?"

"Too late now." Will said.

Chapter: Will

The worst happened. Will had been duly impressed with how quickly the detachment of soldiers got the eight wheeler functioning again, loaded, and headed back down the road. His experience with bureaucracy only extended to his short time as a teacher, and that had been fearsome and terrible with its amount of red tape. Granted, the other teachers were amazing at pulling together in an emergency, but the branches of the tree of administration were heavy laden with the fruit of paperwork.

"Ron, have you ever heard of an IEP meeting?" Will was curious if he could share some experiences with the people he was traveling with. Did they have anything in common except for the current situation?

"A what?" Ron looked down at him from his seat on top of the cargo.

"Never mind."

"My brother had lots." Mai strode next to him. Will mentally noted to use the word strode as he watched her from the corner of his eye. Her walk was a woman with a new purpose. He really wanted to ask her about it, but felt they weren't there yet. Killing aliens on an unknown planet was fine, but talking about private issues seemed wrong somehow, or too soon. "He had dyslexia. There were meetings and arguments with the math teacher. When we got home Mom yelled a lot and called the teacher some bad names." She slowed down and dropped back making it obvious she didn't intend on extending the conversation.

Will really wasn't sure how to deal with Mai. She went from being a great part of the group to be sullen and standoffish. At the moment, however, he didn't feel like he could deal with the problem, if even it was a problem. He had only brought up the topic, really, so the new soldiers wouldn't want to interrupt and ask any embarrassing or damaging questions.

So far they'd been lucky with the questions. Straightforward answers about the situation had answered everything to satisfaction. The soldiers hadn't really cared where they'd come from because everything was obvious. Their comrades in arms had been attacked, and even better, Will and his friends had won. That fact covered over a multitude of questions.

Eventually they broke through the line of trees which marked the edge of the forest and a huge camp came into view. Will realized calling it a camp did it a grave injustice, it was more like a small city. Buildings, which looked hinged so they could be collapsed and moved like a child's playset, were everywhere. Some had flags flying over them. Others had guns mounted on top. Around all of it was a glowing barrier of blue light. He assumed it was the futuristic version of castle walls, and noticed that it seemed to be held together by white poles spaced every few dozen feet.

"Those must be emitters of some kind," Ron whispered to him.

Just glancing at him told Will that Ron was in some kind of sci-fi heaven right now. Aliens swarmed the compound, which was surrounded by an actual force field. "The only thing I can't figure out," he quietly said back to Ron, "is why the monolith we came through is so far away from the camp?"

"Maybe it's not theirs," Mai said.

Will glanced over his shoulder at her, "What do you mean?"

"Well," she paused for a moment to think, "what if the monoliths are kinda generic, or they were built by some group before this and both sides can use them."

"Then," Ron jumped on the idea like a happy terrier, "you don't want to have a possible back door right into the middle of your camp. I bet they were made by some ancient race and these guys just figured out how to use them."

"That sounds suspiciously like a TV show I used to watch." Will said.

"Actually," the voice interrupted from behind causing Ron to jump. He tried his best to act like he was calmly looking around as the voice continued, "the monoliths were a joint venture years back by multiple star systems. The hope was that by building a transportation system we can all use, it would foster a greater sense of community and promote peace."

They'd all stopped and looked back to see a giant of a figure in red trimmed battle gear. Will was sure now the red trim denoted some kind of officer corps, but unlike his red trimmed armor this one had two red stars over the left collarbone. He hesitated to think those two stars were the only difference between the two. For starters this, for lack of a better pronoun Will went with person, towered over them by a good three feet. Will was sure it would have taken at least four of his hands just to circle the person's arm, and their legs were even bigger. He had to step back just to be able to look up at the person's face, and thinking of them as a person was starting to wear out the word person in his mind. The problem was he couldn't tell if it was a he or she or if whatever this race was had those distinctions.

"I am commander Vlask and you three are new recruits from the planet Earth. Am I correct?" The voice rumbled like the hint of a thunderstorm in the distance.

Will nodded and decided to take the lead since he was wearing the red stripes. "Yes sir. We were assigned to move this equipment forward from the monolith back there."

The mountain in armor nodded and looked at the other two, "Blue, you look like you need to say something."

Will wasn't sure who the commander was talking to until he realized he was referring to Ron's armor color. He supposed it was as good a way as any to address someone when you didn't know their name yet.

Ron looked around making sure it was him that was being addressed before saying, "I know I'm new here, and I'm not trying to be sarcastic... Does that even translate? Sarcastic?"

"Yes, I know what you mean," the commander replied and rolled his hand in what must have been the universal gesture for get on with it.

"Right, you said the monoliths were built to foster a sense of peace, but..." Ron looked around and trailed off.

"But here we are at war, is what you're getting at." The commander crossed his arms, looked out over the bustling military city spreading out ahead of them. "That is true, and I don't take any offense at it because I too see the hypocrisy in it all. Unfortunately, at this moment, we really don't have the luxury to banter politics and governmental philosophy, so this is what is going to happen."

The commander looked down at his right wrist and a digital display popped up, reaching over with his left hand he adjusted something on it but Will was too short to see what was going on. It was a new sensation for him since he'd been as tall as or taller than most people all growing up and into adulthood. Eventually the commander stopped poking around and refocused on them. "You three don't seem to be assigned to anyone just yet." Will started to speak up but the commander waved him off and continued, "I really don't care why. What I care about is you are available at a moment when there isn't anyone else. I have a job for you to do, and you're a

46

very balanced platoon with the blue and the gray here. I assume you've had some command experience red?"

All of Will's command experience flashed through his head. A few classes studying things like Alexander's tactics fighting against the Persians, Caesar fighting in Gaul, Patton running his tanks across France, were all he had to pull from. He tried to convince himself that some of his computer games counted as command experience but he couldn't. He didn't want to lie, but at the same time he didn't want to get them caught. "Yes sir, some." He hoped his bland facial expression didn't let anything slip.

"Right, sure." The big alien looked at him for a moment. "It shouldn't matter too much. It's a messenger job. We can't send certain things wirelessly since we can't be sure if they've hacked our system or not, so I need you to take a physical copy of the message to a certain gray on the front lines. Most likely, hopefully, he'll have something for me as well."

A message job, Will thought. It seemed perfect. It would give them an excuse to move around wherever they wanted and, hopefully, find something helpful. "Yes sir. Honestly sir," Will decided to add something to give it all a touch of verisimilitude, "we've never been off our planet, or seen other species before. This is all still a bit crazy, and a message job would be great to give us some time to get acclimated to all of this." None of that was a lie.

The commander nodded, "I could tell." He raised his wrist again and flipped through the display. At that moment a ding sounded in Will's ear and his visor dropped. A green blinking icon alerted him to an incoming message. "There," the commander said, "I've sent you his tracking information since he'll most likely be on the move. The message is sealed and only his command key can open it. Now, off with you."

"Uhm, sir," Mai stepped up and Will was overcome with a sense of vertigo by the difference in height between the nine foot giant and five foot Mai.

"Yes, gray?" The commander had to crane his neck almost to the breaking point to get a look at her.

"We haven't eaten in quite a while."

"Right." He nodded. "Do you see the building with the orange flag over it?"

They all nodded even though Will was certain the commander wasn't looking.

"Head there and get some food in you, but don't hang around. I need you off within the hour."

Will wasn't quite sure what the local equivalent of an hour was, but he also didn't want to hang around any longer than necessary. "Yes sir."

The three of them easily wound their way through the bureaucracy of food service. It seemed to Will that some things never changed no matter what planet you happened to find yourself on. That thought led him to wonder how he'd come so far in his mental space. Just a few short moments ago he was running down a hallway freaking out, and now he was standing in line with a tray of slightly recognizable food while wearing a powered suit of space armor forced on him by an unknown alien race. Looking around, he wondered why he wasn't running around like his hair was on fire. The whole situation was beyond crazy, it was beyond his mental capacity to take it all in and make relevant sense of it all. Maybe that was exactly the point, he thought. It was too much. At some point over the last day he'd made a subconscious decision to take it all in chunks, or just ignore certain things until there was more time or more mental capacity for it.

He could handle a lunch line. He'd been going through lunch lines since he was in kindergarten. Every American, at some time, goes through lunch lines and learns that in a fundamental way they're all the same. Are you waiting in line at Subway? Is it a buffet at the Golden Nugget? Maybe you're waiting for the waffle maker in your university's dining hall. It doesn't matter because at the center of it all they're all the same. In a way, it was comforting to be in the same lunch line here on this unnamed planet. The person waiting at the end was the same guy you had to pay, except in this situation, rather than sliding your debit card, you just held up your right wrist and his console beeped. Once you finished with your strangely shaped fruit, he hoped it was fruit, and some kind of fried thing he mentally called a tater tot, you dropped your tray off on the stack of trays and some poor lower ranked person had to take them away and wash them.

Once they were back outside they headed to the nearest break in the forcefield where they were met by a guard. They started to tell him about their mission when he waved them off and proceeded to scan Will's wrist with something akin to a Star Trek tricorder. It beeped and he waved them through.

None of them talked until they made it to the tree line at which point Ron reached out and grabbed Will by the shoulders, "That was so creepy." He turned to Mai, "Wasn't that creepy? Was it just me?"

"Ron?" Will wasn't sure if he should pat him and try to calm him down or pry his hands off.

"No," Mai said, "I'm with Ron on this one. That was creepy."

"Why?" Will looked from one to the other, still wondering how long Ron was going to hold onto him.

"Why?" Ron shook Will, "Are you blind man?" The force of his words beat on Will like the thump of a bass drum, "I felt like I was back in the high school lunch line, but I was surrounded by aliens. Aliens, Will." Ron leaned forward and stared up into Will's eyes trying to add a physical exclamation point to the statement.

"I checked," Mai said, "and I didn't see another human in the whole place."

"She's right." Ron finally let him go, "I mean, you're right. I looked around too and didn't see anything that even could have been mistaken for a human."

"There was the one guy over by the drinks…"

"Yeah," Ron nodded, "until you saw his back."

"I know, right?" She said, and again Will was struck by Mai's back and forth attitude. She was easily bantering with Ron, but earlier with him it was like talking with a sulking teenager. Maybe it was just him.

Will stepped in between them waving his hands to break the invisible threads bonding them through their shared alien abduction story. "Yes, it was creepy, and come to think of it some of the drinks scared me a little. However, we need to figure out what we're going to do."

Mai nodded, "You mean, are we going to do this mission or are we just going to head out and do our own thing instead."

"Exactly." Will said.

Mai turned and looked back at the base, "If it makes any difference, I didn't see anything that looked like a spaceship."

Ron looked over her shoulder, which wasn't too hard, and tried to search the base, "I have to admit, I didn't even think to look."

Will looked too, "Nether did I. Good job Mai. Not that I need to tell you, I just wanted to point out…" trailing off he realized he wasn't sure if he was supposed to act like an officer or not, and if he was he didn't even know what an officer should say.

"Yeah Mai," Ron punched her lightly on the shoulder, "you rock. Unfortunately, that doesn't answer the question."

"No," Will said, glad to have something to fill the void, "but we do have other options. We can head out to do the mission so no one gets suspicious while at the same time looking for anything useful along the way."

"You would think," Mai turned back to them, "if the monoliths were really made to help with trade and peace and all that, there would be more of them around than just the one we came through."

"True, true," Ron nodded. "So you think the story commander gigantic back there gave us was just a cover up?"

"It didn't really feel like a cover up as much as a recited lesson from grade school." Mai replied.

"Sure, sure." Ron looked around at the trees suspiciously, making Will wonder if the trees could hear them, or maybe, Will thought, Ron just wondered if the trees could hear them. "Like they wanted their kids to think they were amazing and smart when in reality they had nothing to do with building the monoliths and didn't want to admit it."

Will still wasn't sure what was going through Ron's head most of the time. Ron went from serious, and according to his test results mathematically gifted, to comic book nerd depending on the situation. Mai he absolutely hadn't figured out. He still hadn't really confronted her about what had happened back at the eight wheeler, btu there really hadn't been an appropriate moment. Sometimes she was talkative, but mostly with Ron. Other times she seemed downright surly. What she had intimated after that first fight had been totally true. This whole situation was insane, they all knew that. They were all handling it in different ways, and maybe, more than maybe, she was still trying to figure out how to handle it. Try to be normal, or have a mental breakdown. Those did seem to be the only two reasonable options.

Giving a mental shrug Will decided to move on. He would have to figure his new friends out as he went along. At least he hoped they were friends. "So, we head off to look for this gray, which I assume refers to the color of the armor..."

"That means," Ron butted in, "Mai is part badass sniper and a spy."

"So..." Will started to wonder how they would even locate the gray they were after when his visor dropped and lit up. A holographic map overlaid the real world showing a trail heading off to his right and deeper into the woods. "Are you two seeing this?"

"Seeing what?" Mai asked.

His visor blinked a message stating mission information was for officer class only, and before he could finish wondering how to show them where they were going his right wrist started blinking. Lifting it he wondered if he could make the map show up somehow, and like magic a holographic overview of the area blinked to life, glowing over his outstretched wrist. "This is so creepy."

"What?" Ron stepped over and looked at the map, "Did it just do a bunch of stuff with you only halfway thinking about it?"

"Yes," Will reached out with his left hand and poked at the map, causing it to spin slowly. "And as bad as that is, I'm not really sure I can take the time, or the mental space to think about it right now."

"I agree," Mai also had walked over and was looking over the map. "There's only so much brain space for worry right now and while something listening to my thoughts is bad…" She looked at the other two meaningfully.

"We have more pressing issues," Will said, "as well as the fact that there's nothing we can do about the stuff in our heads right now." He looked them both in the eye and when they had nodded their assent he looked back at the map. Their position was marked with three colored circles, one red, one blue, and one gray. Inside each circle was a logo. Will's was a stylized eye, he guessed because he was leading them and needed to see stuff. Ron's looked like a raptor's foot with four sharp talons spread for the kill, presumably because he was going to cause some damage, and while Mai's had a gray outline but the inside of the circle shifted color depending on the angle. Will guessed she could be assigned a lot of different jobs and so was not a single thing.

"Aww," Ron interrupted his thoughts, "Mai's is a rainbow."

Mai's fist shot out faster than Will would have expected, and even though Ron did stagger a bit sideways it didn't look like the solid strike had done any actual damage. A slight smile slid across her face, but Will couldn't tell if it was because she liked the rainbow or she liked hitting Ron. Maybe both.

The trail, marked out on the glowing map, eventually exited the forest and led along the rim of a large canyon. Will noted the canyon was filled with green and red triangles all moving in strange patterns. His visor informed him the green were friendly and the red hostile. He was glad this system accounted for people, like himself, who had no idea what was going on.

"Right," he looked up and once again the map overlaid onto his visor, "we avoid both the friendly and the hostile troops unless we see something helpful, agreed?" Ron shrugged and Mai nodded. With part of a thought the trail marked out on his visor turned a nice blue while the rest of the world was a good natural color. I could really get used to this Will thought.

They meandered their way through the forest for a few minutes before he realized someone should be keeping an eye out for bad guys. The last time they were walking along with the eight wheeler one of them was turned into a smoldering pair of boots. "Mai?"

"Yes sir?"

Will couldn't tell if she'd overlaid the sir part with a veneer of sarcasm or not, so he chose to ignore it. "Could you keep some kind of sensor tuned to make sure we aren't surprised like last time?"

"Some kind of sensor?" She cocked her head quizzically.

"You know," Will had no idea, but assumed with everything else they seemed to be able to do, something like that should exist, "just think of something that would continually scan the surrounding countryside to make sure no bad guys are out there."

"Sure, like… huh, and there it is." Her sarcasm died half formed.

Ron punched her in the shoulder, "Ha! Some amazing thing just showed up on your visor didn't it?"

She rubbed her shoulder even though Will was sure she hadn't felt a thing through her armor, "For your information, yes, and now I have some kind of double ring thing floating in the corner of my vision."

"Hey," Ron turned to Will as they continued to walk, "why'd you ask her to do it? I could've done it without arguing with you."

"Yes," Will nodded, "but it's not your job."

Ron cocked his head, "What do you mean by that?"

"He means," Mai was slowly turning her head and tilting it as if trying to keep a fly in sight, "we each have a job that goes with our designated color scheme. You, my friend, are the muscle."

"And you," Ron looked around trying to figure out what she was looking at, "are what?"

"For right now, she's the eyes." Will said as he pushed aside a branch and exited the forest.

The trees cleared and a meadow stretched away in front of them ending abruptly about one hundred yards ahead. Will's trail led them to the edge and over the side. He assumed there must be a trail leading down into the canyon they'd all seen on the overhead hologram earlier.

As he started forward again Mai grabbed his arm, "My sensor is showing a lot of activity that way."

Will raised his arm and thought about getting the overhead map up again. It resolved itself and centered on their new location. He focused on zooming in to get a better look, but all he could get it to do was show red and blue triangles moving around the canyon floor.

"Well that's not very helpful," Ron said with his head poking over Will's raised arm.

"Does your display show any better detail?" Will asked Mai.

"No, but it does say why."

Will rolled his hand in that same gesture of get on with it.

"Both sides seem to have put up some kind of dampening field so that neither side can get a better shot using," she pointed up, "the overhead cameras."

Ron nodded, "Probably satellites."

"Nah," she said, "I bet they use hot air balloons."

Ron stared at her for a long moment, "Really? You went with hot air balloons?"

"What? They used them in World War One."

Will decided to ignore the two and headed off toward the edge of the canyon. He hoped they would keep up. As he came close to the drop off he realized two things. First, there was a trail cutting off to the right and heading down into the canyon, and second, with the floor of the canyon coming into sight, he decided he really didn't want to go down the trail.

The scene unrolled before him like a science fiction work of art. He assumed the valley was maybe a few miles across, his distance estimation skills were never the best, until his suit specifically told him from one rim to the other was two point five three miles. Will wondered how the suit knew his unit of measurement from a planet on the other side of the galaxy, but then decided it wasn't worth bothering with right now. It was a pretty valley, all things considered. Green grass was highlighted by orange and red trees, and at one end golden crops of some kind waved in the breeze. A home with vehicles parked in front lay almost directly beneath him. A muddy road led away from it in one direction to the fields of crops and in the other direction, he assumed, to the nearest town. It seemed that no matter where you were in the known, or unknown, universe, some things were still the same. People needed to eat, and someone needed to grow the food for them.

Even in food replicator situations someone would still want naturally grown food. Maybe this farmer was getting rich off selling natural organic produce to wealthy socialites.

The pastoral scene was, however, not the reason for his hesitation. Even on his worst day he wasn't afraid of farming, and while tractors had never been his thing as a kid, they weren't going to scare him off. Part of the immediate problem was the drop off. There was a trail, that was true. It cut sharply into the cliff face descending into the valley and, at the best, was two feet wide while being steep enough to worry a mountain goat. Aside from the logistics of getting down to the valley floor was the actual problem.

"Whoa…" Ron stopped beside him and leaned over the edge for a better look.

Mai joined them, put her hands on her hips, seemed to think better of the situation, sat down with her legs dangling over the edge and waved her hand at the valley. "And what are we supposed to do about that."

Will looked back at what she was referring to and wondered the same thing himself. Covering the base of the valley was either the best sci-fi battle he'd ever seen, or the worst possible situation he could imagine for the three of them. Large white vehicles moved slowly across the valley floor and spit glowing blue orbs in a lazy arc toward the other end. Small one seater flying machines zipped quickly over the top of them letting out flashes of alternating white and green either at each other or at the larger ground vehicles. Covering the ground were hundreds of individual soldiers in armor just like theirs. Some were fighting hand to hand, while others flickered as weapons of various kinds tried to kill anyone unfortunate to be in the vicinity. The blue orbs eventually dropped into the crowds with earth shaking force causing dozens of armored figures to go flying in every direction. The colors and technology mixed with the pastoralism of the valley floor made him think of a Battlestar Galactica version of a Thomas Kinkade painting.

Just by looking Will couldn't tell which side was which. The armor and the weapons all blended together in an almost dizzying display of light and destruction. His suit, however, was having no problem telling friend from foe, and when Will focused on the display instead of just looking at the chaos below him it all took on a more orderly shape. There were no real battle lines, but they were focusing their fire and movements to the best extent he could see. In fact, after watching it for a while he started to see a pattern to it all. Waves would break into each other, sometimes forcing one side back, then the other side would push back and the action would all begin again.

"What are they fighting over?" Ron's question was quiet, and didn't seem to expect an answer. For a moment Will agreed with the unspoken assessment. There was nothing here. The farm couldn't have been that important, and there didn't seem to be any kind of resources to gain.

With a thought he called up a map on his display and pulled it back to a larger overhead view, and that was when he saw it. "It's a natural choke point."

"Huh?" Ron glanced over at him.

"They can't get through the forests because it would be too much work and they would be slowed down so much the other side could pick them off easily, so they have to go through the open land of the valley floor. Because the valley narrows down here it makes it a prime location to bottle them up with the least amount of resources."

"But," Ron waved a hand vaguely, "what are they trying to get to?"

Mai stood up, "The base we just came from, and most likely the monolith we came through."

"Exactly," Will said. "The valley leads directly to the base and the base guards the entry point."

"Ahhh," Ron nodded, "Take the weird standing stone and you mess up supply routes or maybe even get a shot at a bigger base."

Will looked over the battle, "I wonder how many…"

"Five thousand on each side," Ron looked at Mai then over at Will, "approximately."

"So," Mai leaned over the edge and looked at the trail snaking its way down, "somehow we have to get down this dinky little trail, around the two giant alien armies with," she paused, "approximately," she looked at Ron, "ten thousand soldiers, and find one gray with some message for the commander back at the base."

"Plus one hundred thirty five tanks, three hundred sixty two flyers, and ten of whatever those things are," Ron pointed to some things in the middle of the fight that looked like car sized robotic spiders.

Will looked over the valley in wonder. For a moment he didn't care about how they were going to find the gray. He didn't even care about how they were going to get home, or even how they were going to survive the next few minutes. His eyes lit up with the glow of laser fire, and he could feel the hair on his arms stand up each time one of the blue orbs detonated. The only word that would come to mind was... marvelous.

Feeling a hand on his shoulder he looked over at Ron, who'd lifted the visor on his helmet. For a moment they locked eyes, Ron nodded and said, "I know, man." Then turning back to the spectacle below them they both just watched.

Then Mai stepped in front of them and waved her arms, "Seriously guys? We need to make a decision here. Do we go after the gray or do we slip by and hope to find something farther on?"

Will shook himself to break the nerd spell he'd fallen under, "Right." Calling up a general map of the area he checked to see what lay beyond the battlefield. Miles of forest stretched away in most directions, except the route through the valley. That way was marked with a multitude of warnings blinking red over others blinking in different shades of red. "If we go around this mess there's nothing but empty forest or a valley full of bad guy stuff. If we could get our hands on some more detailed maps we might be able to make it through the valley of..."

Ron poked his face in front of Will, "The shadow of death?"

"What?" Will said.

"The valley of the shadow of death." Ron repeated. "You know, from the Bible."

"Yes Ron," Mai said, "we get it. We just didn't think it needed to be said right then."

Ron shook his head, "Well, I disagree. If we're going to be headed into mostly certain doom then I think we need to give things appropriate names. I think it makes things more manageable. Especially when you have giant robot spiders possibly trying to kill you."

Mai stepped closer to Ron forcing him to look down awkwardly from his open helmet, "Seriously? I..." She looked over at Will and raised the palms of her hands giving him the unspoken form of what the heck man.

"Anyway," Will raised his right arm and projected the map in the air between the three of them, "Mr. Gray seems to be located not far from here, and I think if we find him, what with his job being to spy on the enemy, he might be able to supply us with the maps we need."

"If we can convince him." Mai added.

"Right, and we need to think of some good reasons for him to do so before we get there so we aren't just winging it." Will said.

"So, where is Mai's mysterious compatriot?" Ron poked at the floating holographic map causing it to slowly rotate.

"Well, we are," their three logos expanded on the map showing them at the edge of the valley, "here, and he is," a simple gray circle showed up on the map and slowly pulsed, "here." From the overhead perspective it didn't look that far away.

Mai looked from the map to the valley behind her and back to the map. Reaching out she rotated it then used her two hands to zoom in on the spot. Sighing she looked up at Will, "You knew where he was didn't you?"

"Yes," Will nodded, "but I wanted you two to see for yourselves so you could make your own decisions."

"What?" Ron looked from the map to the valley below. "Oh…" He pointed behind the enemy's lines at the only structure still standing on that side of the valley.

"Yep," Will lowered his arm turning off the holographic map and all three of them turned to look across the valley at a red barn standing at the edge of a field of golden crops.

In practically any other situation the scene would have been described as idyllic or pastoral. It might even have been the centerpiece of a painting put out by a funeral home who was looking to sell calendars to little old ladies. Here, however, the mood was slightly spoiled by the soldiers in power armor firing off weapons of minor destruction while trying to avoid being vaporized by lasers coming from any one of a select number of futuristic death machines. Actually, thought Will, when you look at it in the right light someone might still paint that picture, just for a different clientele, one more geared to comic book shops.

Ron crossed his arms "So," raising one hand he tapped a gloved finger on his chin, "all we have to do is head down there, avoid being killed by," he stopped tapping his chin and waved his hand at the scene below them, "stuff, make it around the enemy's force, and into the only standing structure for miles around…" Mai cleared her throat and pointed at the farm house on the other end of the valley. "Right," Ron acknowledged, "one of the only standing structures, and find Mr. Gray."

"Exactly." Will said. "Now, as I see it we have two options. First, we can take the straight forward approach, go down this trail, and try to make it through that way."

"Or…" Ron let it hang in the air like a deflating balloon.

"Or," Will continued, "we make our way along the rim of the valley until we're closer to the barn and try to find a way down at that point."

Ron turned and looked at the possible route along the valley's edge. His visor dropped and after a few seconds said, "Eighty three point five."

Mai looked in the same direction then back at Ron, "You lost me there."

"Oh, sorry," he said. "The best scan I can do comes up with an eighty three point five percent chance we break something serious trying to get down from the rim of the valley nearer to the barn, and," he pointed with his chin, "there's someone over there."

"You mean we have better than an eight percent chance of making it?" Will tried to look nonchalant and dropped his visor to do a quick scan of the area Ron had been indicating.

Ron chuckled as his visor came up, "No, I mean we have a seventeen percent chance of making it, and that goes down to around three percent in some areas." He dropped his voice to a whisper, "They scrambled behind that group of rocks when I started looking their way."

Mai's voice trickled through Will helmet, "I have eyes on him, her, or it. I can't really tell since they're in armor with the visor down."

Will looked around and realized Mai had vanished while he and Ron were talking. Glancing over he saw Ron's eyes were wide with a grin spreading across his face. Will read Ron's lips as he silently pointed out how awesome Mai was.

"Mai?"

"Yes?"

"Does the individual of unknown species look dangerous?" Will realized as he was asking the question how ridiculous it was on so many levels. First, they were in the middle of an active futuristic war zone and everything seemed to be dangerous. Ron was dangerous... Probably more so than he intended to be, but still the point was valid. Second, he was now existing in some crazy reality where he really didn't know if the people he was meeting were human or not. Most likely not, when he considered the overall situation.

"Well," she paused, "the armor trim is orange and I don't know what that means, but aside from that I don't see any weapons, and my scan doesn't show anything currently active."

Will looked at Ron who shrugged then he replied back to Mai, "Do any of us know if there's a way to tell the bad guys from the good guys?"

"My suit just tagged them as friendly," Mai replied, "so there must be some kind of signal we can track."

Ron pursed his lips and nodded, "Makes sense. You don't want to accidentally laser your squad mates in the face."

"All right, wherever you are Mai, just keep an eye out while I approach." Will kept his visor down hoping it would show him anything crazy before it happened and began walking toward the collection of rocks the individual was hiding behind. Ron started whistling and when Will looked over at him he just shrugged, smiled and kept whistling. Will gestured for Ron to go around one side and he headed around the other. It wasn't that he wanted to trap them, he just didn't want something crazy happening, but before he could do anything he heard Ron on the other side of the rocks.

"Hi," even with rocks in the way Will could hear Ron trying to be chipper, "my name's Ron."

"Don't shoot me," the voice was feminine and as Will rounded the rocks he saw the individual standing with hands raised, "I wasn't doing anything. I was just looking for… uhh…" she trailed off, trying to think of a good reason to be hiding behind a bunch of rocks.

"No worries," Ron said, "we're not looking to get anyone in trouble. Right, Will?"

She turned to see Will coming up behind her and twitched, obviously realizing she was surrounded. Will raised his visor and put his hands up to show they were empty, while at the same time realizing it didn't matter if his hands were empty since he had guns in his shoulders and his forearms. "Hi," his mind raced trying to think of something to say. Now that he'd decided this person wasn't a threat he just wanted to get back to what they'd been doing.

"You're human!" her visor popped up. "You are human right?"

Will looked into the brown eyes of only the fourth human he'd laid eyes on in the last few days. "Yes," he looked over her shoulder at Ron, "yes we are."

"Praise God," she visibly slumped in her armor. "I haven't seen a friendly face since this all started."

Mai's voice interrupted Will's next response, "I assume everything's fine, and there's no one else around so…"

"Yea," Will replied, "she's human."

The new girl looked perplexed, and Will pointed a thumb over his shoulder at the woods, "We have a friend keeping an eye out. She'll be here in a second."

Ron stepped forward, smiled once he'd made eye contact, and asked, "Who are you, and what are you doing out here?"

She extended her hand, "Guadalupe Rodriguez Villagomez, but you can call me Lupita, and what am I doing here?" Her eyes tried to take in everything around them.

"We know most of the story," Will interrupted before she could launch into a whole thing about her life story from the last few days. He really wasn't in the mood right now to listen to someone else's alien kidnap story. Mainly he just wanted to get on with things.

Ron threw him half a glare, "What he means to say is we know how you were kidnapped and processed. Mainly what are you doing looking down on that?" He gestured to the ongoing laser battle below.

Lupita nodded, "I'm with the quartermaster. Technically I'm supposed to be down there at that farm house keeping track of inventory. You see those flying things?" Ron nodded. "Well," she continued, "they burn through power like crazy and need to come in and get their batteries changed on a regular basis. My job was to keep track of what was coming and going."

Ron gave an over exaggerated confused look, and Will almost lost an eye with how hard his rolled, "But," Ron plowed through Will's eye roll like it wasn't even there, "wouldn't that job be better for a computer to keep track of. I mean, with the number of those flying around and the recharging needed for each…"

"There is a computer keeping track. I guess," she shrugged, "I was the back up plan in case someone blew up the computer."

"So what are you doing up here?" All three of them jumped as Mai's question came from a previously unoccupied space between the rocks. Will squinted and realized Mai's gray armor blended in so well he almost couldn't maker her out.

"Well," Lupita continued slowly tossing a glance at Ron who smiled and nodded as if everything was just hunky dory with the world, "when I realized no one was paying attention I just slipped out the back and followed a trail up here. I was trying to decide what to do next when you three showed up."

"You're in luck," Ron pointed to the sky as if announcing she'd won The Price is Right, "we happen to have a plan and are working on a way of getting home."

"Ron," Mai stepped toward him, "may I have a word with you and Will please."

Ron grinned at Lupita, "Give us just a sec if you could."

Will nodded, knowing exactly what Mai was going to say because it's what he was thinking. She was just getting to it more quickly than he would have. They walked a few steps away and Mai turned to the two of them, "Really Ron?"

"What?" he looked confused.

"Don't give me that," she shot back at him. "It's like you found a stray puppy and you want to save it."

"That's a terrible metaphor," he fired back then shrugged, "but not too far off the mark. She's human…"

"So what," Mai said. "She looks like a basket case that's going to slow us down."

"Mai," Will interjected, "Ron may be a little bit quick on this one, but he is right."

"Oh, sure," she nodded, "I agree, she is human."

"Not that…"

"But yes," Ron interrupted. Will raised an eyebrow at him and he shrugged, "What? She is."

"That's not the point." Will continued, "We have a chance to help one of our own, and in this crazy situation I think we need to consider that."

"Are you ordering us to help her, commander?" Mai locked eyes with Will.

"Really, Mai?" Will held the eye contact, "After what we've been through…"

Mai broke the eye battle off and let out a sigh, "You're right, that was…" she looked from Ron back to Will, "low of me. I'm just…" She shrugged and waved her hands in the air.

Ron put an arm around her shoulders and gave her a side hug. She glared at him and he smiled back, "We're all a bit…" he waggled his head, "off, but that doesn't mean we shouldn't help people when we have the chance."

"All right," she pushed his arm off. "Let's help Lupita."

Collecting their newest member they explained the situation while walking back toward the trail. Will scanned the valley's edge as they went and was reminded of their interrupted conversation about how to get to the barn. The edge was mostly cliff face in that direction and Ron sounded pretty sure they would die trying to get down there.

"What good is amazing space armor if you can't fall off a cliff and not get hurt?"

The question was rhetorical but Ron answered it anyway, "You wouldn't die, but you would break some things which would take time for your suits systems to repair."

"All while the lasers are trying to poke little holes in you." Mai pointed out.

"Right, well, it seems to me," Will stepped toward the edge and looked down at the precarious trail, "as your commanding officer" he looked over at Mai and raised an eyebrow jokingly, "that this is the least of our crazy options."

Lupita came up beside him, "I'm still not too sure about any of this. Why don't we just head off and try to find a way home."

"That's just the problem." Will took a step back and raised his arm. This time the holographic map showed a planet slowing rotating. "According to all the data I have access to, every monolith, or even airport and space port, is under the control of whatever side we are technically fighting for. We know that's not true since the other guys are right down there, but we can assume they control other monoliths and space ships too. If we just wander around we're more likely to get pulled into something by our side or captured by the other side. This way we have a reason for moving around and hopefully by helping Mr. Gray we can get some solid information on where something helpful might be."

"And we're back around to thinking up reasons for him to give it to us." Mai said.

"We all know," Will looked at the three of them, "that I'm not really in charge so if you two can think of some better way of doing this then, please, speak up because I really don't want to go down there if I don't have to." After a few seconds pause, and with no amazing ideas falling from the sky, Will nodded and turned back to the trail. "I guess I'll go first then."

Ron put a hand on his shoulder, "Whatever," he rapped his knuckles on his chest plate, "I've got layers of armor on this suit that could stop an actual tank shell." He stepped in front of Will and headed down the trail.

Will stepped off after him with Lupita right behind him and Mai taking up the rear. He tried to keep his eyes on the trail because at inconvenient moments it would decide to narrow or slant deceivingly toward the edge. The real problem, however, wasn't with the trail. The problem was the battle raging to his left, and getting closer. He found he had a hard time keeping his eyes off the flashes of red lasers and blue white explosions, but after a few close calls with the edge he decided to try harder.

Chaos was something he'd had to professionally get used to. His chosen career was a layered cake of chaos with a dizzying array of flavors and colors. He'd once read somewhere that a teacher had to make more on the spot decisions each day than a surgeon.

Some days it was just the noise. Thirty two kids all talking at a normal volume in a small concrete room would eventually drive anyone slightly crazy. Add a layer of crazy filling to his chaos cake and he'd begun to think this alien war wasn't all that bad. In the one year he'd been a full time teacher, he'd stopped a kid trying to dip chewing tobacco in class and try to pass it off as a fat lip, another kid was caught playing with a butterfly knife under his desk, while at the same time he'd had to lecture them on how to plug in the laptop computers. Seriously, just plug them in. How hard is that? Chaos. He loved being a teacher, at least he thought he did. He loved the literature classes he taught. Macbeth was crazy and cool and he couldn't understand how some students thought it was boring. He loved his advanced world history class where they debated who was more interesting between Genghis Khan, Alexander the Great, or Joan of Arc. However, now, in the back of his mind, there was a mental stutter when he said he loved it.

The chaos around him right now, even with the flashing lasers and death tanks, seemed so straight forward. He could make a battle plan, delegate appropriate jobs to Ron and Mai, then deal with it. Glancing down at the valley floor his mind drew colored lines. His small squad could advance and swing around from the right and hit that group of tank in their flank distracting them enough for that pinned down squad to use it's heavy weapons to knock them out. If anything was going to try and surprise them he would place Mai up on the cliff wall in that overlooking crevice there and… He paused. He did make plans for class and he was good at it, but not like he'd just been thinking. It was like that part of him had grown or changed and had started running on its own. He wasn't quite sure what was going on and really wasn't sure he liked it.

After the third switchback in the trail they'd gotten close enough to hear the clank of mechanized killing machines and after another two switchbacks Will was sure he could feel a kind of pressure in the air each time a blue orb launched across the sky.

"Down!" Mai's scream reverberated in his helmet and his legs seemed to buckle in response to her command. He watched Ron drop to a knee in front of him and raise his left arm where a glimmering blue energy shield expanded from his forearm. Glancing toward the valley to see what Mai had warned them about he watched as three flying machines, in a V formation, flew at them with pulses of light flashing from small tubes located on each side of the control platform. Looking back the few steps to Ron's position he noticed the shield he'd erected was bigger than Ron's body so he scooted up until he was tucked in behind the shimmering blue.

Flashes of light against the shield and louder thumps from up the trail caused showers of dirt and rock to ping off his helmet, letting him know how close the shots had come. The flying scooters, his visor labeled them as Zephyrs but with the handle bar and single seat he really couldn't think of them as anything other than scooters, were peeling away after their laser run on the small unprotected group. Ron's shield flickered off and Will watched as Ron flung himself at the closest scooter, grabbing the vertical pole holding the handlebars, swinging on it, and bringing his feet around at an amazing speed to knock the driver into the air. Watching the armored figure fall the thirty feet or so to the ground, Will wondered if the armor broke the fall or if he just broke.

Turning to check on Mai and Lupita he saw Mai kneeling, and sighting down, a long thin weapon that looked more like a needle than a rifle. A faint whup sound was followed by another driver leaving the seat of his flying scooter and Will made a mental note to not piss off Mai.

"Seriously, Mai," Ron's voice broke over his helmet, "I was going to get that one."

"Really?" she snipped back, "You're going to complain now, in the middle of this?"

"Well, yes," Will watched as Ron, jumping from his current scooter, pointed his right arm and sent the nearest driver shooting backward like he'd been kicked by a very large horse, "you could see it was the closest one to me, so it was my obvious next choice."

"You really think I was paying that much attention?" Mai asked.

"Actually I do." Ron landed on the now vacant scooter, grabbed the handle bars and headed back toward Will.

"Okay," Mai liberated two more scooters as the rest retreated and started taking more evasive action to avoid being shot, "maybe I was kinda keeping score."

Ron jumped off the scooter and landed back on the trail in time to watch it spin out of control and slam into the cliff face. "And?"

"And what?" Mai said.

Ron paused obviously watching the spot where the scooter had crumpled and rolled down to the valley floor. "Battery powered vehicles make for bad explosions," he said to no one in particular before turning back to Mai. "And how many did you get?"

"Three," she replied.

Ron nodded and turned to Will. "What about you tough guy?"

"Me?" Will looked around at the strange battle field. Everything had happened so quickly. Reading history books about Alexander fighting elephants in India didn't really prepare you to fight flying laser wielding scooters. It wasn't that he'd been scared or that he'd frozen in indecision. He'd been so amazed at Ron and Mai that he'd sat back and watched, not even thinking he should be doing anything.

Before he could say anything to defend his lack of action Ron looked around, "Anybody seen Lupita?"

All three of them started searching the trail for any sign of her. It was like she'd just vanished. Ron looked over the edge of the trail assuming she'd fallen off in all the action, but there was nothing down below except one pilot slowly crawling away, and the crashed remains of the scooter Ron had watched hoping it would explode. "I'm not seeing anything," Will said. "What about you guys?"

"Well…" Mai's voice would have been a whisper except it was played over the speaker in his helmet giving it a somewhat ominous sound.

"Well what?" Ron asked.

Will turned and headed back up the trail to where Mai was looking at the cliff face. There was a shadowed outline of a person burned into the dirt and rock, and Will realized the stuff that had dropped onto his helmet while tucked behind Ron's shield might not have all been rock and dirt. He shuddered a bit and turned to Mai, "How did you avoid it?"

She stepped back and flattened herself against the cliff face. Almost instantly she was nearly impossible to see. He only knew she was there because he'd been watching the whole time. She stepped away from the wall, raised her visor, and crossed herself, "I'm sorry

Lupita. I should have remembered you were there, but everything happened so quickly."

Will stepped over to her and put a hand on her shoulder, "I was there too, and I was too busy watching Ron play hop scooter. I should have checked on her."

Ron shook his head, "It was too late by then."

"God guide your soul back home, Guadalupe Rodriguez Villagomez." Mai quietly prayed.

Will nodded, and even though he knew it was important to remember and to mourn in these moments, he couldn't stop thinking they were in a really bad position and needed to get off this open trail. "We need to keep moving, or those guys will come back with reinforcements."

After that, they stopped being safe going down the trail. Will reminded himself he'd been improved back on what he was now thinking of as the mother ship, and he needed to trust in his suit a bit more. He found it hard to really trust any of the technology, or the personal improvements, since they'd been forced on him, and he had no real idea if he was in control of things or if it was just an illusion. Whatever his existential worries he did have to admit that he went down that tiny unstable trail like a boss. Finally, he decided it would be faster and make him less predictable of a target if he just jumped down the switchbacks like a giant ladder rather than running down them. After a few hops his visor told him he was close enough to the ground and nothing would break so he just leaped. For a moment he was certain he'd made a bad decision as his stomach dropped then did an internal flip as he dropped, but when he landed and the only thing he had to do was bend his knees and put out a hand to steady himself he knew it'd been one of the best decisions of his life.

"Super hero landing!" Ron announced gleefully as he dropped into an impressive pose next to Will. He held the pose like some kind of futuristic Greek statue until Mai landed next to them and without so much as a bent leg turned her fall into a calm walk and didn't look back. "That..." Ron stood up, "did you see that?" He pointed at Mai but looked at Will. "She didn't even look back." Shaking his head Ron started off after her, "The really cool superheroes never look back at the explosion."

Will sighed, "Maybe so," he said quietly, knowing their helmets would relay his words directly to their ears, "but real commanders have the map and know the barn isn't in that direction."

Without a word Mai turned and headed back in Will's direction. Ron, however, lost it. His laugh was loud enough that Will's helmet had to auto-dial down the volume to the point he could hear Ron as nature intended.

Once they were back in the shadow of the valley's edge Will checked his map again and they headed off at a quick run to their right making sure to stay as close to the cliff face as possible. Their main objective wasn't to find Mr. Gray as soon as possible, it was to avoid the ongoing conflict to their left. Now that they were on the same level, the noise was almost deafening. Will wondered if he could patch into any of the communication he was sure was going on around him, and with just that thought his visor brought up a plethora of options. He could see individual platoons and their designations all aligned by proximity, until he wondered about usefulness and they rearranged themselves by job description.

"Jump!" Ron's warning wasn't halfway through when Will reacted to it on instinct and launched himself forward and up as hard as he could. He'd zoned out the battle while he dug through the communication options, and was glad someone had been keeping an eye out. His jump, with the added benefit of a run up, propelled him well away from the sparkling blue ball of destruction which had been launched from somewhere out of sight. Will's arm hair stood on end as Ron landed next to him and Mai slightly in front. "Wow," Ron glanced at him as they continued to run, "that would've fried us like," he paused to think about it, "like frying an egg with electricity."

"Ron…" Mai's voice oozed a sarcastic eye roll like play dough through his helmet speakers.

"What? It would have."

"Can that big brain of yours tell us something useful, rather than egg metaphors?" She said.

"Well, since you're just going to make fun of my perfectly good electric fried egg similes," he emphasized the word simile, "I'm not sure my big brain should help."

Will sighed audibly, "Ron, be useful before we all die please."

"Right-O Commander…" he paused and looked over at Will, "Uhm, I hate to admit this, but I have zero memory of your last name."

"I'm not even sure I told you, with everything that's going on," Will replied, "but it's Caine, William Caine."

"Commander Caine," Ron sounded it out like an actor trying on a new identity. "I like it, sounds official. So, Commander Caine, here's my first report. The E-Bods move in very predictable geometric arcs, and unless you are a clueless nincompoop you should never actually get hit by one."

"I'm sorry," Mai popped back into the conversation, "but what's an E-Bod?"

Will silently thanked her for bringing it up before he did as Ron replied, "An electric ball of death. You know, the big blue glowing things that almost killed us back there."

"Right," she hesitated, "sorry about snapping at you about your eggs back there. I'm just…"

"No worries, Mai." Ron let silence fall on them for a few paces, "We're all a bit…" He wobbled a hand back and forth then added, "Everybody jump to the left please."

Will was a bit confused by the awkward statement but when he saw Mai jumping to the left he realized what was going on, dug a foot into the soft farm soil and pushed off, redirecting his forward running momentum into a sideways jump. Their now vacated position lit up with the now recognizable blue crackling light of an E-Bod. "Seriously?" Will said as he landed and restarted his run toward the barn on the other side of the fields. "There is so much wrong with this situation."

"I know, right?" Ron matched his speed and both of them corrected course to catch up with Mai who'd landed slightly more to the left. "I mean, those things are seriously dangerous, but also seriously slow. I don't understand how they expect to hit anybody with them."

"And on top of that," Will gestured out to the main conflict raging loudly to their left, "wouldn't it fry their own guys as much as the bad guys?"

"Who knows," Ron said, "maybe the power signature of the E-Bods is recognized by the individual suits somehow and just grounds through your own guys while frying the bad guys. I mean…" He waved hello to Mai as they caught up with her, "these are aliens with technology we don't understand."

Will turned their course back toward the wall of the valley to keep them from drifting any closer to the main fight. "Granted, but still it seems like a lot of work for something that can be easily avoided."

Ron's voice cut in, "Jump right."

Chapter: Mai

Mai found the situation more than a little amusing. They would run for a while then jump. It all seemed a bit silly, and maybe that was exactly what Will had been getting at. A battle of epic proportions ripped and tore through the landscape to her left. A few jumps brought them closer to it and the scale of it was almost more than Mai could take in. Her helmet visor did it's best to sort out the combatants with soldiers being outlined in differing colors, while others had titles drifting over their head with symbols mixed in. She assumed some of it had to do with rank, but without some kind of key she still wouldn't know how to address them.

Watching out of the corner of her eye she saw one soldier get cut in half by a green laser. The other three next to him returned fire with something she couldn't see, but left bright red holes in the opposing soldier as he dropped from what Mai assumed was a jump he took to get a height advantage. Ahead of them she saw an E-bod connect with some kind of troop transport causing it to explode. The shockwave from the blast knocked all three of them off their feet and Mai didn't stop tumbling until she ran into the wall of the valley. Back on her feet and running again she tried to dodge the largest chunks of dirt and vehicle as they rained from the sky.

The ridiculous nature of the situation slammed into her like a derailed train. She wanted to freak out. Part of her knew that if a car full of people had blown up in front of her back in Portland she would've freaked out. The fact that she was simply running on and jumping over glowing blue balls of energy made her want to start laughing, and that was what truly freaked her out. She was worried her mind wasn't her own anymore. It felt like she was reacting incorrectly, as if she knew how the old Mai would've reacted but couldn't bring herself to be that anymore. Had they changed something in her to make her a better soldier? Had they removed some kind of empathy connection from her brain so she would better be able to kill people she'd never met? Did Ron worry about these things? Did Will?

She'd struggle for a year after graduating, bouncing from one job to the next. Sometimes it was her choice because the job ended up being terrible. Other times it was the job telling her she wasn't the right fit. That was it. That was why she was angry with Will. He hadn't struggled. He was the same age as she was, more or less she thought, and he was in a career using his degree. He was in command, while she was still just the short Asian girl.

"Mai." Will's voice thankfully cut through the miasma slowly falling over her mind.

"What?" She knew she sounded a bit snappy and instantly regretted it, but didn't know what to do about it.

Will's reply jumped right over her tone of voice and she was grateful to him for it, "I have no idea what a Gray is, but you're one of them and our contact is one so maybe you should be our contact person."

She thought about it for a second and realized it was a totally logical thing to suggest, "Sure," she realized she also had no idea what a Gray was, "I have no idea what I'm supposed to say…"

"Maybe," Ron's slightly happy tone of voice never seemed to change and she loved him for it, "you should check with your helmet to see if there's some kind of secret handshake or signal so this other Gray doesn't shoot us on sight."

"Ron," her initial eye roll of a reaction was replaced by a realization that he was infuriatingly right, "I'm not going to admit you have a good idea. Mostly because you led with a secret handshake, and that's ridiculous."

"True, true," Ron replied, "these gloves are way too cumbersome for a good secret handshake."

Mentally she requested any information on ways to initiate contact with a Gray agent and her visor started listing out possibilities with the main one being a digital code, called a handshake, that needed to be sent out. She really didn't want to tell Ron what it was called. Assuming Will would have the code in the mission information he'd been given she started to drift in his direction when she saw him raise his left arm.

"It's just up ahead." Will whispered. Mai assumed the whispering was because there might be bad guys around and whispering was how people dealt with bad guys. She didn't really understand why he felt the need to whisper since they were talking over a closed communication network inside sealed helmets, but whatever made him feel better.

Coming to a stop Mai took a quick survey of the area, just in case. She'd found, over the last few hours, that knowing where your options were before the shooting started was a bonus. Directly in front of them was the barn. It was surprisingly traditional for being on an alien world, and by traditional she meant it looked like a barn to a Thai girl who was not raised on a farm. Off to her right was a stand of what they'd been referring to as trees. She'd found in their first confrontation with the enemy that the branches could hold her weight and give her a good vantage point to shoot from. Yes, she had to admit, the sniper analysis by Ron had been correct, but she didn't have to tell him.

On the other side of the barn, to her left, the valley floor started sharply rising up and becoming a cliff face, but at the base of it, not too far from the barn, was a good cluster of boulders. If necessary she could easily slip in-between those and have multiple excellent firing positions without exposing herself. Aside from those points, and actually because of them, she found she was worried. Somehow she'd gone from filling out resumes in a normal residential life to planning how to get the best shot to put a hole in an alien's head. Mai knew she didn't have the luxury of dwelling on the anxiety this all brought up right now, but she did want to make sure she at least acknowledged it and kept it toward the front of her mind. There was this feeling that if she let it slip she might forget the person she'd been, and then what?

A whump rattled her out of her introspection. She felt it rattle her armor and her visor automatically identified the cause, but she didn't need the help. A red highlighted figure landed among the broken detritus of the barn wall it had just smashed through. Immediately her heads up display marked the prone armor clad figure as part of the enemy force, and Mai came to a conclusion at the same time as she heard Will say, "The Gray is inside. Mai, get to those trees and shoot any bad guys you see. Ron, shield up and head straight toward that guy."

The stand of trees started glowing a faint green to irritatingly let her know where her commander wanted her to go, while at the same time the bad guy, who was struggling back to his feet, was now glowing a faint orange color. She guessed that was to mark where her teammate was headed. Wanting to argue, but finding no good reason to, she headed toward the trees. It was exactly what she'd planned to do anyway, and Will was right in sending her there, but she just didn't like being told what to do.

Her anxiety from a moment ago sprang back with force when she wondered if she'd been this argumentative in what she was now thinking of as her past life. In all the jobs she'd worked in her life there'd always been someone telling her what to do. Never once had she been her own boss, so why was she now finding it grating to take orders from someone, especially when the orders made sense and the person giving the orders was a perfectly reasonable and nice individual?

Out of the corner of her eye, or more precisely highlighted on the edge of her visor, she saw Ron lift his left forearm and with a flash a blue shield half the length of his body was constructed from solid light. He lowered his head and charged the now standing enemy without a moment's hesitation. She envied him.

Getting into the trees she easily hopped onto the lowest branch of the one her display marked as the tallest. Climbing and jumping she quickly made it to the highest branch with enough bulk to support the weight of her armor. She'd been ignoring the crashes and flashes of light from the direction of the barn to better focus on not falling out of the tree. It wasn't that a fall would hurt her, it would just cost time and in a situation with an unknown amount of bad guys time was of the essence.

Popping out her medium range rifle she auto focused her scope on the barn in time to see Ron catch an enemy by the foot as it tried to leap over him. Pivoting, Ron swung the soldier like a bat, and threw him into the air directly in her line of sight. It was ridiculous, she didn't even have to aim. A hole the size of her fist appeared in the center of the enemy's armor when she pulled the trigger, and she made a mental note to ask Ron if he'd tossed him toward her on purpose or if it'd been a lucky coincidence.

After a few more crashes inside the barn, which she assumed came either from Will or the Gray they were trying to contact, she got the all clear from Will. It was followed quickly by, "Mai, be quick, he's hurt and says only a Gray can access the information."

Jumping from the tree she dropped about thirty feet to the ground, "In the mission information you received did it have anything about an access handshake?"

"Let me check."

Mai watched Ron disappear into the barn through the hole in the wall, and a few seconds later she jumped through after him. She caught sight of Will kneeling over a strange figure in flickering armor at the same time as she heard his voice, "I think this is it."

A series of symbols flashed across her visor and her suit acknowledged it as an authentic handshake protocol initiator. She immediately sent it to the prostate figure and received back a single word, "Help…"

Chapter: Ron

Ron watched over Mai's shoulder as the Gray they'd come to talk with stopped flickering. It was the most visual sign of death, outside of a movie, he'd ever seen. The Gray's suit looked like it'd been trying to activate some kind of camouflage but had been too damaged to get it right. The first time Ron had looked, a leg, part of the torso, and one arm had blended seamlessly into the background of the barn. Now it was just a four armed, off white suit of alien armor laying on the dirt floor of a barn.

"Did you get anything?" Will's question was obviously directed at Mai.

"Just a cry for help," she moved over and looked down on the alien figure laying in the dirt.

Ron was again stuck by the insanity of the situation they found themselves in. Here he was, having just finished a life or death battle with lasers, energy shields, and power armor, looking down on a figure with four arms. It was so completely bizarre that he needed to mentally check himself. Over the last hour he'd jumped out of the way of giant energy bombs, fought with laser wielding flying scooters, and... He stopped himself from making another list.

"Is there any way to access his suit to see if the information we're supposed to get is retrievable?" Will asked.

"I, uhm..." Mai hesitated. "I think so, but the damage seems to have caused some kind of extra security measure. The suit is worried bad guys will try to get into its systems."

Ron raised his hand, "I can get it."

Mai and Will looked over at him and Mai said, "I don't know if you should even try."

"What? You don't think I can..."

"It's not that," she quickly cut in, "he's a Gray and I'm a Gray."

"Oh, so you think there's some kind of special connection." That, at least made sense to him.

"Just out of curiosity, why did you even want to try?"

"It's the numbers." He looked down at the prostrate form and knew getting out the hidden data would require some seriously fun numerical acrobatics.

"The numbers?" She looked at him like he might be more alien than the four armed man on the floor.

"What?" He looked at her like she'd kicked him, "I like math."

Will broke in, "As interesting as that is, could you please see what you can do Mai?"

Nodding, she unclenched her fists, and Ron watched as the muscles in her face relaxed one by one. He'd noticed how testy she'd been with Will lately and he really couldn't figure out why. Shrugging he watched as she knelt down next to the deceased Gray. Ron watched as a cord extended from the back of her left glove. She lifted the hand of the Gray and connected the cord to a port in his glove. He and Will waited, wondering what was going on, and if there was something he should be doing to help.

After a few moments she disconnected and leaned back onto her heels. "I have no idea what that's all about."

"What?" Will stepped closer.

"Well," she paused and shook her head, "the suit is spitting gibberish at me and I don't even know what to do with it. I tried sending different access codes at it to see if some super secret Gray thing would unlock it, but I got nothing."

"Sweet." Ron did a fist pump. "Well," he put his hands out placatingly, "not sweet that you couldn't do it, but it's sweet because now I get to try."

"Ron," she stood up, "I'm not sure I even saw any numbers, but you are certainly willing to give it a try."

Stepping up to the body he dropped his visor into place and accessed any information on tapping into another suits system. He wasn't really sure how this would work since he'd only done computer programming with a keyboard and mouse. Would a glowing keyboard float virtually in the air in front of him? Would his visor project cool things for him to manipulate like in Tony Stark's workshop in all the Iron Man movies?

The first thing it did was retract about three layers of armor from the back of his left gauntlet. Apparently Mai's suit was a bit less protected than his. Good to know, he thought. I really am the tank of the group. He watched as the cord extended from the back of his hand like some cobra being charmed from a basket. It was a very strange existential moment knowing he was controlling it with his mind. He made it twist toward him and look at him with the connecting end. When he tilted his head so did it.

"Seriously, Ron..." Mai's voice cut through his moment of USB cord introspection.

74

"Right," the cord straightened out and plunged into the back of the Gray's hand to make the connection, "Sorry. I'll get right to…"

His visor flooded with broken pieces of light. After a moment they resolved themselves into a three dimensional flood of random symbols. His suit seemed to be trying to make some sense of what it was seeing and had independently decided it would be easier to deal with it by using the whole of the visual world. It reminded him of the code in the matrix movies except here they weren't just going vertically. Everything was in shades of blue and white, and nothing was two dimensional. Things floated at random, some getting closer then floating away diagonally, while others zipped by left to right only to sprint off toward the far wall and disappear.

Well, he thought, Mai said it was going to be crazy so I might as well dig in and get to it. The first thing he did was sit down and cross his legs. If he crouched for much longer his feet would fall asleep and that wouldn't help anything. Next, he darkened the world around him by having his visor adjust the colors, and at the same time turned the symbols all white so they would show up better. This way he could focus on what was going on rather than get distracted by things like Will shouting at Mai.

Pausing from looking at the drifting snowstorm of symbols he tuned back into Will just in time to hear, "How many, and from what direction?"

Mai shot back with, "I'm counting at least six. Three there," she pointed to the side of the barn with the hole in it, "and three there," she pointed toward the actual barn door.

"Uhm, guys?" Ron turned to look at Will, "Should I…"

"No," Will waved him off, "we need that information. You keep working on it. Mai and I will keep the area clear."

"No worries," Mai patted him on the head, "I learned a new trick."

Ron watched as her suit shimmered and blended in with the dark red of the barn. "Don't get hurt," he said to where he thought she was, "I'd be," he paused not knowing really how to put it, so he added, "upset."

"I'll try my best." With her voice coming in over his helmet system he really had no idea where she'd gotten off to.

"What?" Will chimed in while he headed toward the barn door, "No goodbye's for me?"

"No offense, but she's cuter."

"No offense taken." Will glanced out the door.

"Aww," Mai's voice seemed far away and had a mix of teasing and sarcasm to it, "you think I'm cute?"

"Ron," Will looked back at him, "get to work."

"Right." He focused back on the world of floating craziness and tried to tune out the fight he knew was about to happen.

Reaching out he started to play with the symbols flying by. He stopped one that looked like the Greek letter for pi, but when he tried to pull it toward him it only moved slightly before some kind of resistance stopped it. Letting it go he thought he saw the others around it tremble, so he reached out and grabbed a different one. This one, surprisingly, was just a triangle. He stared at it for a while assuming it would turn out to be something alien with things scrawled in the empty space that he just couldn't see, but apparently it was just a triangle. When he let this one go he focused on the action of the symbols around it and was certain they moved when he released it.

An explosion pushed him slightly sideways, and with barely a thought his visor returned to real color. To his left he saw Mai standing directly in front of the door with her arms out, but after watching for a moment he realized she wasn't moving. His heart started thumping loud enough he was sure she must be able to hear it over their intercom. He'd almost made the decision to unhook from the Gray to go help when her suit opened fire. Something trying to come through the door was taking heavy fire from Mai, but Ron knew it wasn't going to do any good because he could see the signature blue flicker of a shield. He wasn't positive, but he didn't think Mai had the fire power to punch through one of those in a direct frontal assault. Just then a slim dark figure rose up from the grass growing at the outside edge of the door, raised its hand, and shot something into the back of the advancing figure. The enemy collapsed like a marionette with its strings cut. The dark figure looked around before hopping over the downed enemy and circling to the back of Mai's suit. Waving a hand at it Ron watched as the back of Mai's suit opened like a robotic lotus blossom revealing the inside to be totally Mai-less. The black clad figure looked over her shoulder and waved at him before climbing back inside her suit.

Well, Ron thought to himself as he adjusted his visor back to deal with the swirling symbols, nothing for me to worry about there. Apparently Mai was a ninja bad ass out of her suit as well as in it. Good to know, if he ever felt like making fun of her height. On a separate but related note, that just raised her level of hotness by about a zillion. Maybe, he reasoned as he plucked at another symbol passing by, if he solved this little riddle she might think he was hot too, because, at the moment, this was the best chance he had going for him.

Reaching out he plucked another symbol and watched them vibrate, and a similarity donned on him. Plucking more of them as quickly as he could, he mentally adjusted his suits audio sensors until he finally hit on it, and the similarity turned out to be more than just a coincidence. They were acting like the strings of an instrument. Great, he thought as he mentally patted himself on the back with cheering erupting in his head. It died down quickly as a quieter voice in his brain said, now what?

"So, computer," he whispered to himself, "is there any chance this guy had any music saved on his hard drive?"

The problem with music, he thought to himself, was how subjective it was. Music was all about taste and culture, how you were brought up, what music your parents listened to, did you even like your parents, did this dead alien even have parents the way humanity thought of them. Maybe it was a race of beings like some frogs or plants back on earth that didn't have male or female and just swapped genders. What kind of music would a gender swapping alien reptile listen to? What if he decided to leave his planet and joined up with the galactic navy where his music choices were influenced by other cultures?

His brain was in crazy high gear while he waited for his suit to do a search for anything that could resemble music on the other suits memory. While he waited and watched red negative icons pop up time and again, he mindlessly plucked at the floating strings in front of him. Some part of his brain rebelled at the fact that they were out of order. Higher notes were randomly interspersed throughout the lower notes. He momentarily wondered if that was just how this alien's species decided to roll with it. Maybe their ears were built differently and the notes sounded right to them, but it just bugged him. It's not that he was obsessive compulsive or anything, he just felt the need to organize things.

His suit alerted him to incoming shrapnel and he ducked an arm sized chunk of barn wall. Readjusting his visor to the outside world he watched Will put one hand against the wood of the barn wall. Where his hand touched it the wall blurred into smoke and was sucked into his suit. At the same time he extended his other hand and multiple barrels deployed around his wrist forming a miniature Gatling gun. The barrels started to spin and Ron could hear tiny puffs of air as some kind of projectile exited each barrel at a very high velocity. Will took a step to the left and sucked up more of the barn wall while firing like he was trying to mow down a forest.

Turning his focus back to the problem at hand, Ron saw that his suit had tossed up a total negative on finding anything on the other suit. Turns out the lock he was trying to get through guarded everything on the suit, so even if this guy had some sweet alien tunes he wouldn't be able to access them until he broke the lock. On the positive side of things he'd been able to identify all the notes and after a few tries got them all in order.

When he plucked the last note all the symbols stopped moving, lined up in nice rows, and proceeded to fold themselves into a floating cube of glowing white light. The light wasn't consistent, but was, instead, made up of all the floating symbols pressed together. "Well, well, well. As they say," he whispered to himself, "sometimes it's better to be lucky than good."

Reaching out he spun the cube then realized he probably should have paid attention to where it'd started since that might have meant something. On the other hand, every side looked the same as the others so what harm could he have really done. He tried focusing in on the cube only to discover that every side really was exactly the same, so he then tried just pulling at it. Figuring the only reason to have a cube was to put something in it he poked and prodded at the thing from every angle until finally he saw a change. Putting a hand on opposite sides of it he pressed together. The cube flattened, and when he rotated it, the symbols, now stacked on top of each other, formed words. They weren't words he could understand but he did recognize them as something.

Informing his suit that it would be great if it could translate it he waited for a moment expecting another negative response. Instead what he got was an English transcript floating in the air next to the glowing white square. When he asked his suit, he found out the original language was a fairly standard galactic script used on a few dozen worlds.

His hopes high, he started reading the floating transcript:

"Once there was an island full of shoes, and a little town called Soleville. Living there was a mad scientist called LARRY! He wanted to rule the world, but he didn't have an army, so he conducted a super dangerous experiment. He put a shoe and a blanket into his mixing machine and what came out was the most terrifying creature ever... A SOCK!!!

Larry trembled at the site, "It's a sock!" He trained the sock, but all he could do was dance, so Larry got rid of him. While the sock was on the street he learned how to fly and attack and eat ice cream. One day he heard sirens, so he went toward them and he saw people in black suits. They were robbing the bank!! Jumping into action he knocked the men down, tied them up in a rope, walked out of the building, and did what he did best... Danced right in front of the police and flew away. Now the citizens call him CS (Captain Sock Man). The End."

Ron stared at the words for a moment and realized he now totally understood the definition of the word perplexed. Reading it again he tried to glean some special meaning from it all, and failing that he tried spinning the glowing white square onto different sides to see if the words would change and things would make sense. When nothing changed he started his computer running different permutations of numbers to letters, and after a few moments of getting nowhere with that he decided to ask Mai something.

"Mai?" Not sure if she was in range, or even if the suits had a range, he waited for her to respond. When she didn't answer he thought she might be pulling that whole jump out of your suit trick again so he tried again, "Hello, Mai, come in, it's Ron."

"I'm a bit busy right now." Ron heard a single sharp gunshot in the background.

"Sorry to bother you while you're trying not to die and all, but I had a quick question for you."

"Make it quick. I've got a few seconds until Will brings the other fool back into range."

"So, I've been feeling really weird and super motivated to do things that I normally would do, but now I feel a lot stronger about doing them. Does that make sense?"

"Ron, was that a question?"

"I know it's odd, but does it make sense? Have you been more than you normally are when it comes to feeling certain ways lately?"

"First off, your grammar needs some work. Second, yes."

"Okay, so if there was an opposite to that overpowering emotion what would you say it was right now."

"Hang on."

Ron waited on the other end of the line listening to multiple gunshots and even a few words he was slightly surprised Mai knew. However, they were all adults here, some more so than others, and he wasn't about to give her a hard time about her choice of language while fighting armored aliens with laser rifles.

"Do I really need to talk about my emotions right now Ron?"

"Humor me, I think it's important. He's a Gray, you're a Gray, and I need to know what he might have been thinking."

"Fine. I guess you could say I'm feeling overly serious right now, so the opposite of that would be... I don't know, not serious?"

"So, dancing in the street?"

"Uh, sure, I guess dancing in the street would work."

"Great, thanks."

"Sure?"

Mai's bewildered voice faded into the background as he scanned the transcript again. Finding the right section only took a moment, and asking his suit to line up the English version with the alien stuff written in white letters happened almost before he finished thinking about it. Watching the English words float over and and line up with the alien script he realized the grammatical structure must be fairly similar since nothing about the order of the words changed. Once they were lined up he found the alien word that translated as dance and tapped it. The white glow turned blue and twisted around the word, sinking in like a sideways whirlpool, and with a less than spectacular click his suit informed him he was in. Quickly scanning the contents of the Gray's super secret drive he realized they would need to talk before he dove farther into what was there.

Pumping his fist in the air, he let his visor refocus on the normal world where he saw Will standing over him, and off to the side the back of Mai's suit was open and empty again. Looking around he saw her walking up and brushing dirt off her suit.

"Well," Ron stood up, "that was exciting." He looked over at Mai, "I didn't even know we could get out of our suits like that, and using it as a turret was inspired."

Watching Mai climb back into her suit for a second time he realized she was really cute, and that was unfortunate. Every time he figured out he liked a girl, and he liked Mai, things went poorly. He was too talkative, too much of a nerd, or just too much himself. Not too many years ago he'd tried not being himself to see if that would help, but things went even worse because it's hard not being yourself for any length of time. Eventually he cracked under a massive amount of what he now knew was resentment. He resented his girlfriend for not liking him for who he was. On the positive side it was a learning experience. Once he figured out how much he didn't like being someone else it meant he knew who he was, and that was a good thing. Mai was serious, but that helped balance out his insistent desire to see the crazy in everything. She was cautious while he liked to hit things head on.

Speaking of hitting things, or thinking of hitting things as the case may be since he wasn't really speaking but actually just thinking, even though it was like speaking in his own head, and he wondered if other people thought out loud in their own heads… The point he was trying to make to himself, in his own head, was how he'd really liked hitting things lately. It wasn't out of line with his personality, but it was a little bit much. Lately, it was like he'd said to Mai during the fight, their improvements had taken something about them and turned it up a few notches. He did like to charge in and knock things in the face, but since the aliens had kidnapped them it seemed he thought about it less and did it more. Mentally he shrugged, then, with a mental picture of himself shrugging, he wondered if other people pictured themselves in their heads shrugging or did they just know somehow that they were doing it in their sub conscience without actually needing to do it consciously?

"Well?"

"What?" Ron looked over at Will.

"Ron," Mai stepped up, "you zoned out there for a bit."

"Oh, sorry." He mentally pictured himself tossing aside a magazine with all his worries in it and pulling up a digital readout with all the information he'd just gotten. "With everything going on, there's a lot crowding my brainy parts right now."

"Tell me about it." Will and Mai said at the same time.

"Jinx," Ron said.

"Really?" Mai raised an eyebrow and tossed him a half smile.

"And now you owe me a soda." He paused, "Or do you call it a pop? Or a coke? Or a soda pop?"

"Ron." Will gave him his patented Commander Caine look, or at least Ron thought it should have been patented.

"Right. There's multiple issues going on at the same time so let me try to put them in some kind of order." He looked at the ceiling for a moment and shuffled things around on his mental digital display. "Okay, most importantly is what the information actually is. It's a list of all the known monoliths and where they go."

"Seriously!" Will did a double fist pump. "Is there a way home in there?"

Ron shrugged and raised his hands, palms up, "That's where we come to the second issue."

"Which is…" Mai waved a hand for him to continue.

"I'm not sure if there's a way home in there," before they could say anything he raised a hand to stall any response, "I can't go through all the data because it's too much for my suit to download and search through, so unless either of you have some extra memory capacity, we'll need to break it up into chunks between the three of us."

"Well…" Mai dropped her visor, "I do have some extended memory capacity, but it looks like the dead guy got extra because of the mission he was on."

Will nodded and dropped his visor into place, "It looks like I can drop all the info from this mission and free up some more space. There seems to be a good chunk of memory in here for command stuff so…" He stopped, "Someone's coming." He turned and pointed to the hole in the wall.

Ron reflexively dropped his visor and started mentally warming up his weapons of minor destruction when his heads up display marked the incoming person as friendly, and a medic.

Will waved his hand at Ron, "Stand down."

"What?" Trying to act casual he mentally told the two shoulder cannons to get back into his suit, "You two just got to blow up a bunch of stuff. I felt a little left out."

Another armored figure stepped through the hole in the wall. This one was smaller than the three of them and had green trim. Ron noticed there were no extra arms or spider legs. As far as he could tell, it was basically human.

Will stepped up and flipped his helmet open, "Hi, you're a medic right?"

The newcomer tapped their helmet and the entire thing telescoped back and into the suit, revealing a blue skinned female, or at least what Ron assumed was a female. He had to keep second guessing himself since everything around here was literally alien. Her features were thin and delicate. He noted that she had normal facial features with two eyes, two ears, her nose and mouth were in the right place, and she had the right proportions. She had a liberal dose of black freckles over her nose that emphasized her one non-human fact. Her skin was blue. Trying to give it a name he ran straight past powder blue, that choice was too light, but not quite all the way up to royal or navy blue, those were too dark. Her hair was definitely the darker variety of blue, almost black. It was in a single braid and long enough that it disappeared down the back of her suit. Looking at her eyes Ron realized he was going to need to revise his earlier thought about her only non-human trait. The color of her eyes reminded him of his cat he had growing up. It was a yellow somewhere between gold and orange. The pupils were the normal human round shape and there were whites around her irises which was helpful and made him feel like things were a little less weird.

"I'm the medic for the six seventy first engineer battalion. I saw there was an injury in need of immediate care and, being the closest, I headed this was a fast as I could." She looked around until her eyes fell on the Gray sprawled on the floor of the barn. Will stepped out of the way as she walked over and knelt down.

As she looked over the fallen soldier Will looked over at Mai then made eye contact with him. Ron shrugged. They were on a legitimate mission. He was fairly sure she would just confirm the guy was dead and move on to rejoin whatever group she'd been with. It didn't seem too likely a medic could tell them what to do, but again they were on an alien world and for all he knew she could be the princess.

Mai waved a hand at Will for him to do something. She gave him this look that was an entire paragraph about him being the commander so why didn't he act like it in the one situation where they needed him to. Ron was impressed with how much she could fit into a look. He was also impressed with himself for reading it.

"Is there anything you can do?" Ron wasn't sure it was the best thing for Will to ask, but at least he was being honest.

She looked up at him from a display she'd been using to scan the Gray, "Not here, but maybe back at the med tent. It really depends on how long it takes to get him back."

A message popped up on Ron's visor. It was a request from Mai's suit. Scanning through it he saw Mai had been able to make a wireless connection with the Gray's suit now that Ron had brought down the digital security. He agreed to her suggestion and the download started. Reaching up he tapped Will on the shoulder, "Sir, there's a message."

Will dropped his visor then nodded in Ron and Mai's direction. When the transfer was done they would all have approximately one third of the map. Now they really had a reason to stick together.

"Commander?"

Will flipped his visor back up and looked at the medic, "Yes?"

Ron could tell Will, like himself, had no idea how to address other soldiers. What made it even worse was there was no common reference. Back on earth he could at least take a stab at rank structure simply because of all the movies they'd all watched at some time. Here, however, there was none of that. Who knew what the ranks were called here. Maybe princess was a rank. If so, would he be prince Ron?

"Linka-Lucina," she extended her hand, "I believe this is how humans greet each other?"

Will shook her hand. "Linka-Lucina is your name?"

"Sorry, yes." She let go of his hand, "My suit's telling me this all has to do with some mission I don't have clearance for."

"That is correct." Will nodded.

"And I was right that you're human?" She asked.

"Yes…" Will's voice faltered somewhere between an answer to her question and asking a question himself.

Ron was a little concerned about the direction the conversation was taking, but obviously not as concerned as Mai was. He could see her from the corner of his eye as she shifted position. At first he wasn't sure why, but then realized it was so Mai's shot wouldn't go through the new girl and also hit Will. That was very thoughtful of her. Murderous, but still thoughtful.

"So you were conscripted?" Linka-Lucina asked.

"Depends on what exactly you mean by conscripted?" Will responded.

"Big ships showed up at your planet and kidnapped you."

Will said, "Yep, that's what happened."

Ron nodded along and said, "Well, after the creepy alien message that went out trying to convince us it was all for the good of something or other."

Linka-Lucina looked over at him and nodded a greeting, "Bruiser."

Ron nodded back and smiled. Bruiser. He liked that. It fit with how he felt lately. Then he realized his visor was still down and there was no way she could see him smile, so he flipped it up and gave a smile again.

Over his headphones, on the private group channel, Mai very quietly yelled at him, "Don't smile at her. You don't know her. She might be finding out how we feel about her galactic overlords so she knows if she has clearance to kill us all."

His eyes flicked from the blue skinned alien to Mai and he whispered back, "Really? I'm just trying to be friendly? And, anyway,

84

I thought it was my job to come up with seriously crazy conspiracy theories. Are you feeling okay?”

“I...” Mai paused, and he heard a serious sigh, “Like someone said earlier, I’ve just got a lot going on in my head right now.”

“You gonna be okay?” Ron didn’t have to try, the concern in his voice was genuine.

“Are any of us at this point?” Mai answered.

Ron totally agreed with that sentiment, but at the moment there was nothing he could do, or say, to help Mai. He tuned back into the conversation between the alien girl and Will.

“So,” Will was saying, “did they improve you too?”

“I’m not quite sure what you mean by that, but I don’t remember any statements to that effect.” Lenka-Lucina replied. “What I do know, is that it was not by choice and I would really love to find my way home. The problem,” she shrugged, “the problem is I don’t know where that is or how to get there.”

“Will,” Mai whispered over the group chat, “she could be pumping you for information to see if we’re loyal or not.”

“Mai,” Ron looked right at her.

“What?” Mai shot Ron a look, “I’m not being paranoid, just cautious. I don’t want to give away what we’re doing and lose our best chance at getting home.”

Lenka-Lucina raised her hands in a pacifying gesture, “I know I’m being really forward about this, but I don’t have a lot of time before they expect me back. Let me be clear about this and you can check if you want. I’m a medic, there is nothing I can do to stop a commander on a mission, and there’s especially nothing I can do to interrupt a Gray on a mission. I was kidnapped from my home and my family, like you were. I want to get home. I’m hoping a group of humans out here on their own might know something I don’t, and might not be so happy to serve in a war they know nothing about.”

“Well...” Will raised his hand and put up one finger, “I’m going to need a moment with my squad.” He walked off to the far side of the barn and waved for the others to join him.

Ron noticed Mai keeping the new girl in line of site so, just to play devil's advocate, he turned his back to her. A message chimed for him so he lowered his visor to see that the download from the Gray was almost finished. Will paced toward the barn wall and back, “Pros and cons friends.”

Mai pointed at Linka-Lucina, “She’s not human.”

Will nodded, and Ron understood the implied meaning. The medic could be working for the bad guys. The only real way to know she wasn't, if she was really a she, would be if she was a human. He wanted to present a balance to Mai's argument but at the moment he had nothing so he queried his suit about the new girl's species and history.

Will shrugged and said, "Not to sound cliche but that's a bit racist, and just because she isn't like us doesn't mean we shouldn't help her."

"Her story sounds too made up and convenient." Mai responded.

"But," Will continued to pace, "if they really were onto us enough to send someone then why send her with a too convenient story. Why not just send a squad that has the ability to turn our suits off?"

"Maybe they're not sure. I mean, we are on an official mission. She might not have been officially sent. Maybe she's like a form of secret police and there's one of her in every unit to make sure everyone is loyal to the cause."

Ron continued to listen in as the information he requested scrolled in front of his eyes. Both Will and Mai were making good points. Granted, they both had a lot of maybe's thrown in there, but in an open discussion that was a good thing. Off to the side of his current information, a green target box popped up showing a friendly squad coming their way. Mai and Will stopped discussing. Mai turned to the medic and Ron knew that if she turned out to be a threat Mai would handle it, so her turned toward the incoming squad. Hopefully they wouldn't need to shoot their way out since, as they had said so many times before, they were on an actual mission.

Linka-Lucina stepped toward them, "They're going to want to recover the body. What should I tell them?"

Will nodded, "We were tasked with recovering sensitive information from him. We did, and now we need to get that information back to a place and person that we can't tell you about." He stepped up to her and put his hand on her shoulder, "I'm sorry." With that he turned and headed toward a hole they'd busted in the barn during the fighting. "Let's go."

Ron turned toward the medic and raised a hand, "Good luck." He meant it and after reading what information there was available on his suit he truly felt bad for her.

Chapter: Will

Will decided the best thing to do would be to run. At the moment he had no specific destination in mind as long as it was opposite from all that stuff in the canyon. The choke point of the canyon eventually widened out and Mai yelled at them. Will stopped and looked at her.

"Reinforcements are coming up." She pointed ahead.

Will used his visor to zoom in and saw the leading edge of new enemy forces coming up through the cleared portion of the forest. "Mai, what's the closest cover for us to avoid contact with that?"

She pointed off to the right where the valley's rim was now a gently sloping edge leading up to the main forest. Will turned on his best speed and after a few moments asked his suit how fast they were going. The visor showed them hitting a good seventy miles per hour. Over his intercom he heard Ron give out a whoop and assumed he was checking their speed as well. The difference between the two of them was Will was also checking how long they could maintain this speed. He knew they could momentarily push themselves a little faster, and Mai, with a lighter suit, could most likely beat them all, but they could only maintain this for a few hundred more yards before needing to slow. Thankfully the woods were only a few hundred more yards ahead.

Once in the cover of the trees Will realizes he hasn't been thinking about this the right way, "The trees don't matter."

"What?" Guns popped from Ron's suit and attempted to point in every direction at the same time.

"Sorry," Will said, "I mean, if we can sense bad guys coming through walls and down in canyons from a distance then why did I think these trees would hide us?" Shaking his head in disgust, "We just need some time to get a look at these maps and figure a way home."

"I think," Mai paused as if looking at something, "I think I might have a temporary solution." The right shoulder blade of her suit folded open and a triangular drone flew out then started to ascend until it reached just above tree top height. "That should block our signals, giving us some privacy for a little bit. If they get too close they can still figure out if we're here, but normal passive scans will pass right over us."

Ron flipped his visor up and grinned, "I love having a super spy sniper on our side. Now what I really want to know is…" He trailed off and stared silently into the woods for a moment. "Nope. No drones in my suit. Apparently they don't carry enough fire power for me. That's actually kinda disappointing."

"Awww…" Mai reached up and patted Ron on top of his head.

"Wow," Ron looked down at her, "you are so short."

A click made Ron look up in time to see Mai's drone hovering over his head with a small laser pointed at his face. "She says differently."

"She?"

"Absolutely."

Still staring down the little triangle of death Ron said, "Just because you're small doesn't mean I don't think you're really cute, and strong, and smart, because…" He trailed off and blushed.

"It's all right," Mai said as she waved the drone back to its position above the treetops, "I think you're kinda cute too."

"Uhm…" Ron looked at her, obviously struggling with what to say.

"Okay," Will's voice cracked the tension building up between them like a hammer hitting ice, "I've found the first step, but after that I don't seem to have the right data."

Ron and Mai looked over at him. Will realized he'd been standing off to the side quietly looking through the data on purpose. He'd been hoping something would come up between them, not because he was a great judge of character and he knew they would like each other, but because he liked them both and wanted them to be happy. He'd been able to tell for a while now that Ron had a thing for Mai. He did the traditional high school guy thing of bumbling about when she was around, or saying random things because his brain broke when she looked at him. On the redeeming side Will could tell Ron was mature enough to know acting a certain way wasn't going to work, and he was proud of Ron for just continuing to be himself. Mai on the other hand was really hard to read. When they'd first met he thought he had her pegged, but as the mission went on it turned out he'd been wrong. What really bothered him right now was the fact that he'd just called this a mission. Apparently he was really getting into this commander role.

His short time running a high school classroom had come with some command benefits. You had to be comfortable telling people what to do. Admittedly, it was easier telling young idiots what to do than telling grown up equals what to do, but the same principles still applied. What he needed now was a little bit of time to plan. Being a beginning teacher he'd relied on time to plan things out and then time to look back on those plans and modify them to work better next time. So far in this mission there'd been no time to plan, just act, and definitely no time to reflect on how things had gone. It was time to plan. He took a deep breath and pulled up a holographic display of the local map he'd been going over on his visor.

The others walked over, Ron was obviously glad for the interruption. "We are here." A red X marked their current location, "Over here is the nearest monolith." His map zoomed out and a green dotted line led from the red X through the woods to a clearing. The clearing was marked with orange and yellow buildings, designating which ones were dangerous versus which ones were just enemy buildings. In the middle of it all, surrounded by barricades of various kinds, was the monolith. "It's obviously not controlled by our side which poses a problem."

Ron reached over and changed the perspective of the hologram to show the enemy forces marching into the canyon, "With all their attention focused on breaking through the valley I suggest we simply rush them. I doubt they'd be expecting it, and since we aren't trying to take over the base we don't have to worry about securing anything."

"I was generally thinking the same thing," Will responded. "We just need to find the best direction so we have less chance of getting killed on the way. Mai, what do you think?"

Mai leaned toward the map and at the same time a figure burst from the underbrush behind her. Leaping nearly six feet into the air and spinning toward the target Mai whipped out a rifle. Will jumped in-between waving his arms and yelled, "Don't shoot! Stand down!"

Mai's rifle kicked and a tree behind and just to the left of the emerging figure cracked in half. Landing, Mai yelled back, "What is going on? Why am I not killing them?"

Will, in the middle of the insanity, was seriously impressed and a little let down all at the same time. Mai had responded to the threat, and on top of that, had actually listened to him when he yelled at her. On the other hand Ron was just standing there. They could all be under fire or dead at this point and Ron was still figuring things out.

"Hey, Lucy," Ron waved at the newcomer. "Took you long enough."

Her visor flipped up showing her blue face and black freckles, "Lucy?"

"Look," Ron shrugged, "Linka-Lucina was just too long to say, and since I know lots of people are going to be shooting at us I shortened it down out of pure survival instinct."

She thought about it for a moment then returned his shrug, "Considering everything right now, sure, that's fine."

Will realized, in that moment, he may have been thinking about Ron the wrong way the whole time. He assumed Ron hadn't reacted because he was a slow brute. He was their muscle, their tank. Maybe, however, he'd figured this all out faster than himself or Mai and just saw no reason to react.

"What, the high holy eff is going on here?" Mai, still pointing her rifle at Lucy, looked over at Ron and Will. "How did she know where we were, and," letting go of her rifle with one hand she pointed at Ron, "how did you know she was going to be here?"

"Oh," Ron nodded as if she'd made a valid point in an argument, "I didn't know she was going to be here. I just made a best guess based on the information available. Mainly that our commander here is a big softy."

Will realized he'd made a mistake not telling the others what he'd done. Just when he thought he was getting this commander thing down he went and missed something important, namely, communication. "I felt like she was telling the truth and gave her my transponder code so she could find me after we left the barn."

"I looked up her story," Ron chimed in quickly before Mai could point her rifle at Will, "and everything she was saying came back true. Also, most of her people were killed when they resisted the conscription efforts. She's one of the few survivors."

Will felt himself untensing and grinning at Ron. Cool under pressure, and Mai could really bring the pressure, he'd taken the initiative to look up the relevant information. Will raised his hands in a mild gesture of surrender, "Mai, please put the gun away. I'm sorry I didn't communicate properly. That's on me."

"Yes, Will, it is." The rifle disappeared somewhere in her suit. "We..."

"This has all been great," Lucy interrupted, "but my squad is going to be really pissed that I took off and their most likely coming after me right now."

"Did you turn off your locator beacon?" Will asked.

"My what?" Lucy looked down at her suit as if a blinking button would appear to help her out.

Mai rolled her eyes, "Seriously?" Turning she glared at Will, "She's going to lead them right to us. She may not have been a danger, but now she is."

"Look," Will stepped toward Lucy, "just pull up a file on your visor called locator beacon functions. Then re-assign its squad designation to the one I'm sending you. That way we can find you and they can't." He turned to Mai, "Will your disruptor drone block them from finding us?"

"No," her rifle reappeared, "it's designed to keep bad guys from accidentally finding you, not to keep your own squad from tracking your location." Mai held up a hand to stop Will from asking her a question, "My girl just did a long range sweep and there's a group of friendly soldiers headed this way at a high rate of speed."

"We really need to find a way to designate everyone except us as bad guys." Ron said as he turned in the direction Lucy had come from.

Will's mind spun for a moment then settled. He'd never really liked being in charge, but he'd learned how. What it came down to, for him at least, was realizing that a decision had to be made. You could worry about the impact of the decision and try to see if the outcome would be good or bad, but when it came to the proverbial point of the sword you had to make the decision. At that moment he felt like Indiana Jones stepping off the cliff in the Last Crusade. He didn't know if there was an invisible bridge to catch him, but he really hoped there was. "Well," he looked at Ron, "it looks like the plan will have to go into effect immediately." He gestured and they started to run toward the next monolith. Mai and Ron reacted immediately with Lucy jumping and trying to catch up. "Mai, can you get an overview of the camp up ahead and find us the best direction for attack?"

"You mean while I run through this forest?"

"You always said you wanted a challenge."

"No, actually, I never said that. Ron, did I ever say that?"

Ron dodged to the right of a tree, "I'm going to have to side with Mai on this one, but I will say that the spirit of the statement is true."

"See," Will jumped over a small ravine with a creek at the bottom, "Ron agrees with me."

"He did not." Mai shot back.

"Guys," Lucy voice came over their intercoms strained and breathing hard, "this is all really fun banter but I can't keep going this fast, and would someone please tell me what's going on?"

"Oh," Will slowed, "Mai?" He left the question unsaid.

"Yes, Commander Caine, I've got it covered." With that Mai disappeared into the woods ahead of them, and Will knew she would have a route scouted out when they got there. She might have even taken out most of the guards too. He realized he didn't mind that, and it kind of worried him. He didn't remember being this callous with lives before. A few of his students could have been run over by a bus and he wouldn't have minded, but casually noting that Mai was going to snipe some unknown people was a little strange.

"Lucy," he was grateful to Ron in that moment for giving her a nickname, "give me permission to check your suit systems." They'd slowed to a jog and he realized for the first time that he was feeling thirsty. A straw extended from the right side of his helmet and he sucked some water through it. At the same time a chime let him know he'd been granted permission to mess around in Lucy's suit.

His commander status gave him certain access to his squad's systems anyway, but his had been augmented by the mission parameters that had been set for him when they'd been sent to find the Gray. He kept one eye on the wooded terrain in front of him, hoping Ron would yell at him if something really bad was about to happen, while at the same time he dove through system menus in Lucy's suit. Eventually he found the problem, or more accurately problems. First, it turned out, she wasn't improved like they were. He didn't know why, or what that implied, but she was all natural. This meant she literally couldn't keep up with them when they were running flat out. Second, her suit had been limited because of what her job was. You didn't need your medic to have all the bells and whistles turned on since she was basically going to be standing around helping you not die.

Running down the list Will ticked any box that wasn't ticked. Some things he wasn't sure what they did, or if they would be helpful, but he didn't want to take the time to do research either so on they went. "Hey, Ron…"

"Yes sir, Commander sir?" Ron was obviously not out of breath or out of sarcasm.

"Check through your suits sub systems to see if all your abilities are switched on. If it won't let you then let me know and I'll do it for you with my command override."

"Check."

"Lucy?" Will looked over at her, but couldn't tell anything since her visor was down.

"Still here," she said between heavy breaths.

"I'm about to flip a switch. It should make your suit pick up a lot more of the slack and help you keep up without killing yourself." He took a second to scan through the list again to make sure he hadn't missed anything, then, basically, pushed the submit button at the bottom. He watched the system cycle through the new commands then received a happy little chime saying everything was good to go.

Lucy shot ahead of him, almost tumbling over, "Whoa!"

"And she's off." Ron laughed as he caught up to her.

"Anything on you're suit Ron?" Will asked as he caught up with the two of them.

"Just a few fail safes and limiters. Things they tossed in there to help you not kill yourself."

"We don't need those." Will said with what he hoped was a heavy dose of sarcasm in his voice.

"Nah," Ron replied, "if anyone's going to kill us, it's going to be Mai. Also," Ron turned and started to run backward, easily keeping pace with Lucy and Will, "I was taking a look through the monolith information I downloaded."

"Seriously?" Lucy's breath came rough and fast, "Are you just showing off?"

"A little, yes."

Will couldn't see Ron grinning behind his tinted visor but knew it was happening.

"So," Lucy slowed to jump a fallen tree, grunted with the landing, then continued, "it was monolith entry and exit information you got from the Gray?"

"Yes," Will replied before Ron could. He didn't cut him off for any particular reason, but Ron already had Mai to banter with and didn't really think it would be fair if he also got to do all the banter with Lucy too. The problem was, his ability to do witty banter wasn't the best, and with his promotion to commander it seemed to have retreated even farther. Being a commander wasn't about chit chat with your squad. It was about making sure everyone was taken care of, doing their job, and headed in the right direction. Thinking about it now, he realized that wasn't really like him. He'd been okay at leading before being kidnapped by aliens, but not this single minded about it. It was, again, a bit worrying. However, running through the forest, being chased by angry highly weaponized aliens, and trying to impress a pretty blue skinned girl, wasn't really the time to get all metacognitive about life.

"So," Will tried again, "we were sent on a mission to retrieve whatever information that Gray had."

"That part was true?" Lucy glanced at him.

"It was why we were able to move around without anybody giving us a hard time. We could, legitimately, say we were on a mission. When we arrived at his position is when we realized he was holding all the secrets to the monolith locations and where they led to."

"And that," Ron jumped over a creek while still running backward, "is where you came in, and why I started looking through the data for where to go."

"The first monolith," Will cut back in and simultaneously wondered how Ron was even able to see what was behind him, "was in my information but not the one directly after that."

"Which is where I come back in…"

"Commander," Mai's voice cut into the conversation.

"What is it?" Will responded.

"Incoming plan." Mai said.

Will slowed as Mai's plan of attack popped up in his field of view. It had them swinging part way around the camp to the right and entering through a gate on that side. The visuals showed light resistance at that gate with supplies coming into the base through there. Once through, things got more complicated with different possibilities marked out in varying colors of difficulty. One plan looked better than the rest just because of the sheer surprise of it. He marked it as the most favorable and sent it out to the rest of the squad.

"Really?" Ron turned forward again and ran next to Will.

"Yes, really."

"All right. I approve of this plan."

"I thought you would. Anyway," Will turned their speed up again and started curving his route to the right like Mai's plan called for, "what were you saying about the next monolith?"

"I have the location of it, but not where it goes from there. We really need a moment to coordinate what we know so we're not just jumping randomly."

Will nodded, "I was kinda hoping we would find some kind of control allowing us chose a specific location and jump right to where we wanted to go."

"Yeah," Ron said, "but that would make way too much sense. I'm really starting to think these aliens have no clue how the monoliths work."

"Right?" Will nodded vigorously. "Unfortunately their lack of knowledge is really starting to impact our ability to get home."

Lucy was sounding better after the brief slow down, "I studied the monoliths a bit before being snatched up. It seems, as best we can all tell, they're fixed points and can't be changed."

"Speaking of points," Will looked over his shoulder, "most of your squad has dropped off, but some of them are being seriously persistent."

"Also speaking of persistent," Mai's voice poked back into the conversation, "I've needed to go pee for the last hour."

"Seriously?" Ron replied. "Just go in your suit. It has a whole system for it. I've gone pee three times already. It's very convenient."

"Really, Ron?" Will could hear the tinge of disgust in Mai's voice.

"What? We've been running and getting shot at. When was I supposed to climb out of this suit to take a leak? I still haven't had the guts to go number two." Ron chuckled to himself, "Get it? Had the guts?"

"Ron…" Mai, Will, and even Lucy's voice blended together in response.

Thankfully, to Will's commander sensibilities, the edge of the trees was just in front of them and Mai dropped from one of the last ones and fell in behind Ron. The walls of the base were easily visible now that the trees were gone. The bottom six feet were made of blue metal with a projected force field extending from the top and forming a dome over the whole encampment. The only break in the fortifications was the gate that was now directly in front of them. Mai's reconnaissance had shown a barricade that could be closed to lock the entire base down in case of an attack, but it had also shown the local guard was relaxed and not prepared to jump into action.

Glancing up Will noted Mai's helpful little drone zipping overhead doing its best to block the fact that bad guys were currently sprinting directly at the only opening. "Remember to collect your drone before we jump through the monolith." It didn't cause him to pause, but a part of his brain did politely take the time to point out how strange that statement was.

"You don't have to remind me." Mai responded.

Will knew he didn't need to remind her, but something commander-ish inside of him made him do it anyway. Just like what he was about to say to Ron, "Ron, you remember what you need to do?"

"Absolutely Commander Will sir." Ron didn't sound annoyed that Will had reminded him. "And also sir," Ron added, "may I just say how much I appreciate this chance to show my helpfulness, and usefulness to the squad."

This time Will couldn't help but smile. Knowing what was coming, and knowing how much Ron was looking forward to it, made him feel like a good commander. They ran straight past the pair of gate guards, and Will's smile turned a little wicked as his fist shot out and connected with the left guards visor at full speed. A subconscious check showed he was going seventy four miles per hour which made his punch connect like Thor's hammer to the face. He wasn't sure what happened to his right but a crash followed by Mai's voice informed him the guard on that side was taken care of as well. A flash of metal caught his attention and a quick glance showed Mai's drone coming home. It seemed there wasn't much it could do to cloak their presence now.

Alarms began blaring and flashing lights matched the high pitched shriek. "All right Ron, you're up."

"You don't have to tell me twice!" Ron's shout of joy matched the intensity of the alarms as thrusters on the back of his suit fired up and sent him flying over the nearest structures. At the apex of his jump the thrusters held him there for a moment, but that was all he needed. Ron turned into the Devil's own fireworks display. Shoulder mounted rockets fired in two different directions while wrist mounted lasers swept an arc of burning destruction to the left and right. As the rockets detonated, Will, Mai, and Lucy were leaping their way in a direct line to the monolith. Will had looked over Mai's possible routes and decided going down any of the preplanned roads was going to be difficult. The base would have defenses set up in those areas, but it was likely those same defenses wouldn't be set up to fire directly over their own buildings. As a bonus this was a more direct route.

Will glanced back to see Ron rise from the smoke and flames of his own chaos. This time his blue shield was up deflecting incoming rounds of both laser weapons and conventional bullets. From the back of his suit, where Mai's drone lived, something akin to a gatling gun extended. As Ron hung there for a moment, supported by his thrusters, the gatling swiveled almost faster than his eyes could track.

96

Each time it paused, a deep grunt, like a giant trying to lift a building, was directly followed by something being torn apart. At the same time, more shoulder mounted rockets pored indiscriminately into the base around them.

As Will leapt again he found himself matching Ron's whoop. Catching sight of the monolith rising up he felt compelled to remind Mai of her job, "Mai, remove the guards before they do something irritating please." The please at the end was added to make sure she didn't take this precious time to argue with him.

"My pleasure boss." Her response was quiet, calm. It was actually kind of eerie, with the explosions and mayhem of Ron behind him, to see Mai in front of him dropping guards like they were pesky mosquitoes. Every time she rose above the buildings another group was trying to make it to the monolith, and that same group would drop like spilled toy soldiers. It did, however, have it's own cool factor. Ron's show of force was all bright and shouty, but Mai's was just as deadly, and scarier in its own way. The real triumph, to him, was that she hadn't argued with him. Maybe it was just the heat of the moment, and knowing there was no time for it, or maybe the action itself was flipping switches inside them and they were now just the roles they were designed to play. He was the commander, Ron was the muscle, Mai was the snipper, and now Lucy was the medic. In this moment it felt, if he took the time to look inside himself, like he wasn't Will, he was just the commander. The loss of control, even if it was simply a perceived loss, bothered him. It wasn't that he was a control freak, or even that he enjoyed being in charge, it was this situation. All control had been stripped from him. He'd been taken from his home, forced through processing, jammed into this armor. Even his thoughts and actions were seeming more and more to be pre-programmed. It all bothered him.

It didn't bother him enough to forget his duty to Ron, and as he landed on top of the last building leading to the gray standing stone waiting to transport them across the galaxy he shot a message out, "Ron, I'm in position. Get your fiery butt of death over here." He took a knee on the rooftop and popped out his largest gun to cover Ron's retreat. He wasn't as equipped as Ron, at least when it came to weaponry, but as they always said, it's not the size of the gun, it's how you use it that really matters. He had one shoulder mounted rocket pod, and using his visor he ordered it to self track any targets coming from his left and take them out with prejudice. At the same time the right side of his visor was tracking and locking on targets for his rifle.

Slight shifts in his grip and stance allowed him to pull the trigger the moment a target lock turned from yellow to red. Most dropped with one shot, but some took a bit more of a pounding, or more tactical shots to take down.

Will knew Ron was on his way by the trail of smoke and screams he left behind. He hadn't been shooting at anyone or anything in particular. His mission had been simple, cause chaos to help cover their advance. If enough things were blowing up and burning they would be less likely to mount a single devastating defense against the squad as they ran through. Ron had been smart enough to make most of his explosions happen farther away in the camp. There were buildings burning at the far edge, and as his shoulder rocket took out another incoming hostile Will watched one of Ron's rockets fly off and drop on the far side of the mess hall. The command part of his brain told him this would be a serious benefit to the war effort back in the canyon. Those reinforcement they had seen headed up the canyon would either have to pause and wait to find out what was going on, or they would be called back to deal with what they perceived as a massive assault on their base. Either way, it would save the day for their side.

Calling them "their side" didn't sit well with him. The thought had popped into his head without his approval, and Will wasn't happy with it. When they had a moment he really wanted to talk with Mai and Ron about whatever was going on inside his brain. Currently, however, Ron was bouncing past him and Mai and Lucy were kneeling at either side of the monolith with guns raised. They were close enough to it that the warping effect of the monolith caused them to stretch in odd ways, and made Will wonder if they'd be able to shoot straight. When he'd initially sent out the plan he did say Lucy was to help hold the entry area with Mai, but he had more imagined her simply waiting there while Mai did all the gun work. Not because he thought of Lucy as less of a soldier, but because he didn't know if medics even carried a weapon.

"Lucy," Will landed and started running toward them, "medics have a gun?"

"I'm as surprised as you are." She and Mai continued to survey the area but no more soldiers came into view, "I guess when you unlocked all that stuff a gun was part of that."

Ron slowed and three weapons on his suit swiveled in different directions looking for anything to shoot, "I would guess the suits are all fairly standard with mostly the same equipment."

Will and Ron came to a stop at the edge of the monolith's influence, "All right," Will looked at his little squad, his visor showing him the mission had taken less than three minutes, "we don't know what's happening on the other side. They might have sent a message through. Which means we might be landing in the middle of badness. Ron." he turned and looked at the squads muscle, "how you doing on ammo?"

"Fifty percent."

Will turned to his sniper, "Mai?"

"Eighty percent."

Finally his medic, "Lucy?"

"I shot one person in the leg."

"I think she did it on purpose." Mai said.

"Yes," Lucy responded. "I did. I don't like killing people."

Mai's grunt had notes of respect in it, and Will decided he could wait to sort out any possible issue between those two. "All right, Ron you lead. Shoot anything that moves. I'm bringing up the rear. Lucy be ready to patch any of us up." A chorus of yes sirs greeted him as Ron turned, yelled something, and disappeared into the monolith.

Chapter: Mai

Mai had decided a while back that the aliens in charge of this war were idiots. At first she'd been giving them the benefit of the doubt because, well, just because. Because everything was happening so fast, because she couldn't see all parts of the situation, because they had advanced technology, and because if they really were idiots then a lot of things ceased to make sense. The problem was, things didn't make sense. Why kidnap them instead of building robots? If they could make power suits this amazing why not just build an army of robots? Why let them wander off and not even have some kind of tracking device on them? Finally, the most recent issue, why hadn't the base they'd just burned their way through sent a warning message to the exit area of the monolith? Also, were these two monoliths connected by some crazy science or were they the same monolith pinning down a point like a thumbtack through a folded piece of paper? That was a thought best left to math boy Ron or commander Will. She had more gun related things to keep track of.

Thinking of those two, or more correctly thinking of the three of them, as a team was a little strange. She'd never been part of a team, at least not like this. Each of them was at a transition point in life. A spot where you have to step out onto the trapeze rope with no net to catch you. Ron was the youngest but had a serious plan for his life, she was a bit older than him but was totally floundering when it came to life, and Will was on the real deal career path. Maybe it was those different perspectives that gave their little team the strength to make it through all this crazy.

She'd totally agreed with Will before they'd jumped through the monolith. There should've been someone waiting for them on the other side ready to turn them to dust as they emerged. They would have been sitting ducks. It was almost ridiculously unguarded and Ron hadn't even felt the need to blow anything up. He actually looked sad when he said he'd rather conserve ammo for when it was needed than blow up a bunch of aliens who didn't seem to know what was going on.

That didn't stop Mai from taking out one alien. He'd been about to access some big communications array, and since she didn't know what he was going to say, or if he was about to call in a bunch of reinforcements, she shot him. It amazed her how easy it had become. See a problem? Shoot it. In her previous life that hadn't been an option. Bad relationship? Guy turns out to be a jerk? Shoot him. Yeah, that didn't really fly. Part of the problem was how close you were to the issue. She didn't know the poor alien she'd just taken down. He was just doing his job. He might have been kidnapped from his home planet just like her. Maybe if she'd taken the time to get to know him they would have been great friends, but now she'd shot him. Really, she didn't feel bad about it, and that kind of made her feel bad about it.

"Mai," Will's voice broke her train of thought, "Ron and I don't have the location of the next monolith. Check your data please."

It was nice he was saying please, and she'd definitely become more comfortable taking orders from him. Her visor turned the data into a three dimensional construct floating in front of her as she ran. She'd heard Will say he was looking for a place to settle in and get a grip on the situation, but she really didn't need to pay attention to that. It was Will's job to deal with that stuff. She just needed to shoot things, and currently figure out where they were going next.

The data showed three monoliths within a moderate distance of them and one on the other side of the planet. It was a strange moment. Looking at the distance to the monoliths she had to decide how badly she wanted to get home, and at what distance did things become too far. Would she be willing to head toward the monolith on the other side of the planet if it would get her home? How long would it take to get there? Was she willing to spend a year or more in this suit, missing her twenty third birthday, running from aliens, and fighting for her life just to make it one jump closer to home? The real problem was she wasn't sure which would take them closer to home. The map showed labels floating over them, which she assumed were the names of the planets, or places, they were linked to. She shot that information to Will and Ron asking if they knew which one would be the best case. For a moment she hesitated then decided to send the same info to Lucy just in case she knew anything about the three possibilities.

Waiting for Will and Ron to respond she decided to actually take a look around. Right after they came through the monolith she'd just followed Ron. Turns out she kinda liked having a brick of a guy in front of her. It made her feel comfortable. It wasn't just the fact that he was muscle in a powered, heavily weaponized space suit, it was his personality. He grinned. Not just smiled, but grinned. Part of her was starting to feel, how could she put it, depressed. She shot things, so did he, but he had fun doing it. There was more to it than that, and yes, she admitted to herself, those few moments they'd had to joke with each other had been nice. He was cute, and funny, and smart, and wasn't she supposed to be taking in the terrain?

Shaking her head the drone popped from her back and zipped up a few hundred feet. It's video feed and data popped up in her field of vision, while at the same time she just looked around. Apparently, the monolith had spit them out in some alien version of Nevada. Scrub brush lightly dotted the area with a lonely tree holding out against the universe every once in a while. The trees that did exist were short, and that was saying something coming from her. The bark was a grayish brown that was wind polished to a silvery sheen in places, with the leaves being an ashen green. To her right the ground didn't so much rise up as crash up. It looked like a solid rectangle of stone simply popped up. Intellectually she knew it had something to do with erosion getting rid of the soft layers while denser stone stayed put. "Ron? Is it denser or more dense?"

"What?"

"If I were to take the time out of my crazy, aliens are chasing me life, and look at the landscape, would you say the stone leftover around us is denser or more dense?"

"Well," Ron's voice took on a far away quality, "since you asked the question, it depends. You can talk about a city having a dense population in which case the comparative form of it would be denser or densest. However, when comparing the density of two substances like liquids or in this case rock you would use more dense."

Part of her brain said it was a great metaphor for how she should look at life. Let the non important stuff blow away and hold onto what was important, but really it just looked like a giant toddler had dropped a building block.

"Will," she'd seen something through the drone's eyes, "there's something you should see." With a thought she shared the video feed with Will's suit. What she was seeing was familiar in some ways, but certain things about it were just bizarre. She really hoped they weren't headed to the other side of the upthrust mountain because once again the red and blue lasers of a full blown battle were blocking their way.

"Right," Will didn't sound worried, "any caves up there for us to take a moment in?"

Mai asked her little friend to take a look and the results came back quickly. There was an indent in the cliff face about two thirds of the way up. It was deep enough for them to effectively remain unseen

102

from anyone below and she could have Dorothy, the name for her drone had just popped into her head and she liked it, cover their electronic signatures. Marking the spot and sending it out to the others Mai turned toward the cliff. From the data Dorothy sent, it was a good couple hundred feet up from their current position, but there were enough hand holds that it shouldn't be a problem to get up there.

On the other hand, "Ron?"

"Yes, my dear?"

She wasn't quite sure about the "my dear" part, but she let it slide for now, "You think you could give me a boost up please."

"You want me," he turned and looked at her, "to throw you up there?"

"Yes, please."

"Why?"

"First," she reached over her right shoulder and pulled out her favorite rifle, "I would like to be up there while you all climb up so I can make sure no one is following us. Second," She slowed and motioned for him to get there before her, "it just looks like fun."

Ron's visor popped up and he shot her that grin she loved as he sped up. Maybe, she thought, this is why he grins. The aliens were idiots, they were in the middle of a galactic war, but they could at least take the fun moments when they came. Smell the proverbial roses. Ron came to a stop at the base of the cliff directly below the cave. Crouching down he put his hands together in front of himself. Mai had never been in a situation where someone had needed to throw her over anything, but she had needed to be boosted up to get things so many times she'd lost count. Being short was annoying sometimes. This time had nothing to do with being short. Refusing to slow down she planted her left foot in the palms of his interlaced hands at a dead run. Ron lifted up with his arms, jumped, and fired his boosters for a second, and Mai found herself flying.

Once they were all up Will, of course, had to remind them not to step on the mud brick ruins filling most of the cavern. Mai didn't care so much, but Will kept going on about how one circular depression reminded him completely of something called a Kiva from Colorado. They finally sat down and started comparing notes and found to their annoyance a complex network of monoliths that didn't seem to be helpful in the least.

Shaking her head, Mai wasn't sure why someone would even invent this network. The technology itself was amazing. It created the ability to go directly from one planet to the other without the time spent in-between, but you couldn't choose where you went. On the one hand, her economic lessons came back and told her these monoliths made trade much more possible, but on the other hand her practical side kicked in and said if you could only trade with the ones directly connected to you then the benefit was marginal at best. What if you produced warm woolen coats and the planet you were connected to was comprised of hot deserts? Not very helpful.

"Got it." Mai looked over at Ron, who she thought had zoned out like she had. He waved his hands and a holographic web of blue lines popped up connecting glowing purple stone monoliths. "You can't get there from here," One monolith blinked to show where they currently were, "and, from what I can tell, there's only one working monolith in our home solar system."

"Is it on Earth?" Will sounded incredulous, and Mai thought of all those standing stones scattered around Europe. At this point she wouldn't be surprised if one of them turned out to be active. She pictured them popping out into some small Irish village dressed up in their gigantic alien power armor.

"Nope." Ron reached out and zoomed the map in on the last one in his marked out line. Their familiar solar system came into focus with the large gas giants circling the outer rim of the system. Just inside the orbit of the giants was a ring of debris, and the purple highlighted monolith was blinking on the biggest chunk. "That," Ron waved dramatically, "is the dwarf planet Ceres. A few years ago NASA put a satellite in orbit around it and immediately was amazed by a very bright light shining from the bottom of a giant crater. They told the world it was a crystalline salt structure which had been exposed by whatever asteroid plowed into it and made the crater. Turns out it was an alien base with an active monolith creating a galaxy spanning wormhole in it."

"So," Will leaned closer to the hologram, "I'm hearing two things. First, we can't actually get there…"

"Well…" Ron wiggled his hands noncommittally.

"We'll circle back around to that," Will replied. "Second, even if we do get there we have to find a way to get from Ceres back to Earth, which means a ship of some kind."

Third, Mai thought to herself, there's a standing stone on a dwarf planet, asteroid thing, put there by aliens way in the past that can transport stuff from another solar system. Why would they do that? Why not put it on Earth? Had they been watching them?

Ron nodded and interrupted her thoughts, "True."

Will turned to their medic, "Lucy?"

Her visor was up and she'd been looking at the ruins around them. They were uniformly brown because they seemed to be made entirely of local wood and mud bricks. There were no ceilings, most likely because they were inside a cave which provided a natural ceiling for everyone.

"Lucy?" Will repeated.

"Oh, sorry, I was zoning out there a bit." She replied.

"Do you have any idea how to fly a spaceship?" Will asked.

She shrugged and shook her head, "I don't."

Mai's brain did a double take. It wasn't the fact that a medic couldn't fly a spaceship. That was to be expected. It was Lucy's attitude that bothered her. She had jumped into this group on the premise that they could work together to get home, but her home wasn't even in the same part of the galaxy as theirs. If they made it home, to Earth, how would that help her?

Will let out a deep sigh and his visor flipped up, "Look," he leaned forward and put a hand on Lucy's shoulder, "I'm sorry we haven't been looking for a way to get you home too. I was so focused on us that it totally slipped my mind that making it back to Earth wasn't going to be helpful for you at all."

Lucy looked him in the eyes and nodded, "I understand. You find your people a way home and if a chance comes for me we'll figure it out."

Ron leaned in and broke the eye contact, "No worries Commander. I've got you covered."

Mai shook her head. Ron could be adorable, but at the same time that happy energy caused him to be so oblivious some times.

Waving his hands, Ron zoomed back out away from Earth's home system. Making a swiping motion with his right hand, he spun the holographic image then grabbed it to make it stop. "I give you the answer to our first problem, and Lucy's problem, all in one." Zooming in they saw groupings of multiple monoliths. They were arranged in rings of six each, with each ring being only slightly off from each of the others. "I call it the nexus."

Once Ron had identified the hub, what Mai called her new brain started working overtime. Back in the previous world, when she wore makeup instead of armor, she'd just survived at work. It wasn't that she didn't care it was just nothing really special, it was just work. She knew she had a good knack for planning and what the business world called managing, but her problem was she really didn't like working with people. Her ability was in creating the roadmaps, the big picture, not in making sure everyone around her was appropriately doing their job. Her new brain seemed to have taken this skill, or idea, or dream, and dialed it up. Now she automatically saw pathways. She saw not just how she would go, but how each of them could make the best use of the terrain or cover. Will would need to be able to have a good overall sense of the situation so he would need to be central while Ron only cared what was right in front of him so he should be up front. As she looked at the map showing the Ron named nexus her new brain spun out multiple options for how to get there. On the one hand, she hated it because she felt like it wasn't really her. Thoughts came up that she wasn't sure she had thought. On the other hand, she was really good at it and for once in her life she didn't feel short.

Her job wasn't argued over. Mai told them the best route and they nodded at her. She knew once she'd done her job Will and Ron, and hopefully Lucy would do theirs. If things fell apart it wasn't their fault, but she was prepared for that as well. Now that the path was planned, her job was to look over the terrain and see if there were any traps along the way. Traps could be anything from narrow points where it would be easy to pin them down, areas with too much cover where the bad guys could surprise them, or known battle grounds that were overly hazardous to their health.

Their first goal was at least partially helpful, in that it was the closest of the three monoliths on this world. She was glad it hadn't been the farthest one. In that case they would've needed to cross an ocean. Mai didn't even want to think about how hard that would have been. The part that wasn't helpful came back into view as they crested the top of the cliff above the cave.

"Sand worms..." Ron's voice was weighed down with such a sense of awe that his words dropped like rocks. "There are laser blasting, power armor wearing, aliens riding on giant sand worms." He turned to Mai and pulled her into a hug. "I can die happy now."

Groaning, she wrapped one arm around him and patted his back. She was fairly sure, if his visor had been up, she would have seen tears in his eyes. Letting her go, but keeping one hand on her shoulder so he could apparently shake her anytime he saw something cool, she was free to take in the whole situation. It wasn't as confined as the battle of the valley. That had presented its own problems. With no way to effectively go around, they'd needed to expose themselves to unnecessary danger. Here the battle was spread out over an open desert landscape. It reminded her of the one time she'd driven to Las

106

Vegas. Chunks of brown and reddish rock a few hundred yards long stuck up from the scrub brush covered landscape, but most of the area was generally flat and dry. She noticed a sand dune or two scattered here and there, but nothing that was more than twenty feet high.

The battle itself was, as Ron was proving with his pointing and squeezing of her shoulder, a nerd's dream. Giant brown segmented worms undulated like snakes across the desert landscape. Each one had what she could only call a driver at the front end followed by two to three different weapon possibilities farther on. One had mounted cannons on top that acted like anti aircraft guns, while another had multiple smaller guns all along the sides firing down at ground troops. Part of her said the long monsters could just as easily be snakes, but the lack of scales and the general brown sliminess cemented them in her mind as worms.

Will rapped his knuckles on Ron's helmet to get his attention back on the group then turned to her, "What's our best play, Mai?"

"They don't have any eyes."

Will looked at her, "What?"

"How do they…"

"Well," Ron chimed in, completely ignoring Will exasperated sighing, "if they're anything like earth worms then they would have light sensors to tell them when it's dark or light out and they can sense vibration to tell them what's around them. Also," he waggled his fingers at the crazy milieu before them, "they do have pilots that must have some method of control."

"Come on you two," Will stepped into Ron and Mai's line of vision, "I think even Lucy rolled her eyes at that."

"Sorry," said Mai, and part of her was. The soldier part of her that seemed to be growing stronger each second was really giving her a hard time. "You wanted to know the best way. There." She pointed to the sand dunes she'd seen off to the left. "There's a dry creek bed headed…"

The explosion threw them all sideways and Mai's brief confusion was overtaken by her new brain. Her suit helped too. Auto repair systems kicked in and her rifle was in her hand as she rolled and finally slid to a stop against the only tree.

"You are under arrest for desertion." A voice boomed as if put on loudspeaker. "Under article eight five of the uniform code of military justice I am bringing this medic in and the rest of you for conspiring to help." Mai's rifle locked onto his helmet but showed the armor was too strong at that point. Her visor suggested his shin. It wouldn't kill him, but it would slow him down. "If you refuse to come with me I have the legal right to terminate you immediately."

"I am on a lawful mission." Will was up on one knee with his rifle painting a red dot on the newcomer's chest, "This medic was requisitioned under my authority..."

"Stop right there," the new guy raised his left hand while his right held a very large gun aimed at Ron who was, with his multiple rockets and guns poking out everywhere, the most obvious threat. "My network informed me your mission was to report back to base with information. Here you are, not headed back to base. Come back now and maybe the commander will hear your side."

Will's shoulders slumped a little and Mai knew what was coming next. Her nice quiet little plan to sneak around the battle below was going right down the toilet. "Sorry," Will said, then followed it with, "Ron..."

Multiple projectiles launched from Ron's suit while Mai rapid fired at the new guy's shin. Only a few hit as he used his boosters to shift left and up in rapid succession. Mai was not surprised when four more armored soldiers popped up from below the edge of the clifftop. Of course he wouldn't come alone, Mai thought.

"Retreat," Will's voice was strangely calm as he backed toward the far edge of the cliff. "Ron, cover us. Mai, find us a new way to the jump point. Lucy, how do we resupply with ammo?"

Mai was very interested in the last question but was too busy trying to dodge laser fire and rockets while simultaneously looking for a new, faster path to the monolith. "Will, we need to cut through the middle of the fight."

"I thought we were trying to not get killed." His response had a strange double sound as they both jumped off the edge of the cliff at the same time. Ron made a few more things blow up then followed them over the edge.

Mai took one more shot as she landed and noted there would be one less soldier chasing them. "We can use the fighting for cover, and, hopefully, someone will shoot those guys behind us."

"Ron, report."

Ron jogged along with his gatling gun pointed backward, "Three left after Mai's parting gift."

"Lucy?"

A cable extended from Lucy's suit to Will's and Mai assumed it was doing some medic thing. "Pick up rocks as you run and tell your suit to use the raw material."

Mai remembered the last two times they'd gotten into a fight and how they'd disintegrated pieces from trees or the barn to allow the suit to repair itself. Bending as she ran she grabbed a rock slightly bigger than a softball and watched it turn to dust and disappear. A lovely chime sounded from her suit and a list came up of things she needed more material for. It seemed she'd taken some damage without realizing it. Scooping up more rocks she watched the list check itself off until only one red message was left. Mai didn't realize her side was hurting until she read the report on how she'd been shot. Then Lucy was there hooking up to her suit and something happened to make the pain go away and the message turned from red to yellow.

"There," Lucy's voice came over her helmet audio, "give that a bit of time and it will seal the wound up and regrow any needed tissue."

"Uh," Mai wasn't too sure how she felt about something unknown regrowing her tissue while she ran, "thanks."

They hit the edge of the battle like running into a wall. The sound and light were almost overwhelming and her visor had to dim itself to keep her eyes from constantly getting spots and streaks. Ron's sandworms weren't just sliding around, they were constantly lifting themselves up and slamming back to the ground. Flashes of light marked laser fire, but unlike the movies you couldn't see the bolts of light fly through the air. Her visor tried to keep up with the origins of the laser fire and calculate the probable path of it, which, mathematically speaking, wasn't too hard since a bolt of light wasn't going to curve for any reason. Separately the thump of solid rounds and rocket fire was followed by rock and bits of scrub brush falling from the sky like the constant pitter patter of horrible rain.

Mai started to wonder if this had been a good idea. Maybe it would have been better to just face off against the remaining three military police behind the dunes. Her thought, originally, was they could just run right through this mess without much worry as long as they didn't try to engage, while mister MP and his bunch would get caught up shooting at all the people they called the enemy. This, however, was chaos. She wasn't sure the soldiers around them were actually shooting at the enemy or if they were just shooting and hoping they hit something. The infantry cannons on the side of the sand worms were totally indiscriminate. They laid down a solid wall of laser and conventional fire. Anyone, friend or foe, who got close enough was shredded or melted depending on what hit them.

Mai's new brain instincts kicked in and she dodged left as a round tore a trench in the ground she'd been running over. Her rifle, now thankfully refilled, twitched up and returned fire. Above her, miniature flying saucers zipped and tried to take down the drivers of the sand worms. Apparently they weren't against taking a pot shot or two at random ground forces either. Her revenge shot amazed even her. Somehow she'd noted the direction the saucer was traveling and at what speed. She'd adjusted and dropped the pilot in one pull of the trigger. Mostly this new self Mai'd become was just an improvement on what she'd already been. Things were just taken and turned up, but the ability to hit a moving target above her was something new, and while a lot of this worried her it also was seriously impressive. She was, against some of her judgement, becoming less worried and more glad with her new life.

"Did you see that Will?" Ron yelled from her left. "I don't even think she was looking when she did that." Some type of shotgun in Ron's right hand kicked and tore a soldier in half who'd been falling from the sky, while at the same time the gatling gun on his back tracked and downed three separate targets coming up behind them in the space of two breaths. His left forearm served as the base for his blue shield, which stretched almost as tall as he was and about three feet wide. Ripples of light on it showed where laser fire and conventional rounds were bouncing off. His shoulder fire rockets were up but not firing. Mai guessed he was saving those for things big enough to need a good boom.

Mai's aim swiveled down and right where a low flying saucer was on an attack approach. This one was easy, coming right at her like that. It did have a shield like Ron's directly in front of the driver which led her to remember something. Jumping as hard as her short, but alien enhanced legs would let her she then used the small booster rockets to give her a bit more height and fired down on the driver. Her momentum met the saucer's and she pushed off its edge with one foot. While in the air she saw two troupers waiting up ahead with what looked like rocket launchers pointed at her squad. By the time she managed to land, at a run, next to Will they weren't an issue any more.

"How do you even know who you're shooting?" Will asked while pushing Lucy slightly left to avoid being shot. "Ron?" Ron dropped back to let his shield help cover her. Will gestured around them, "They could be human. I mean," he looked back over his shoulder to check on the MP's, "they mostly look like they could be human."

110

He was, as he'd said, mostly right when it came to that, Mai thought. Most of the soldiers around them had two arms, two legs, and a head in the right place. Some didn't. "They shot at me first."

"That's," Will paused. "Well, that's actually reasonable. I'll give you that one." Spinning to face the other way, Will pushed her with his left hand while raising the gun in his right and opening fire on the closest MP. The MP dodged to the side while the next one jumped over him, most likely hoping to catch Will unaware. Mai's shot caught him in the chest, and while it didn't kill him it knocked him backward. With one sliding on his back in the dirt, Will connected his rifle to his suit and went full auto on the one who'd dodged earlier. Mai had found the built in weapons didn't need to be reloaded, but the external rifles, like her sniper rifle, could only hold so many rounds. Will seemed to have found the best of both worlds by somehow feeding ammo directly from his suit reserves into his rifle. "Stay with Ron," Will yelled, "I need to slow the guys down a bit."

Taking another shot at the MP who was getting up, she was happy to see him tumble through the dirt again. Catching up with Ron and Lucy, Mai checked over her shoulder in time to see Will use his boosters to dislodge himself from something on the end of the MP's arm, while at the same time sticking something to the guy's helmet. A few moments later an explosion accompanied Will landed next to her, his boosters cutting out, and his legs pumping to keep up. She assumed the unlucky soldier behind them had found out the hard way what Will had stuck to his helmet.

"Will…" he waved her question away, and with no time to stop and grill him about taking an alien sword to the side she let it go.

"Hey," Ron yelled, raising his arm shield, deflected something about the size of a bottle of soda. The detonation behind them told Mai what it was. Glancing over at them Ron said, "I have an idea," and Mai could almost hear him smile when he said it. He obviously had no idea Will had just been injured or he would've asked about it. "Lucy," Ron said as they boosted over a group of ground soldiers fighting hand to hand. A few of them made the mistake of taking shots at them and Mai repaid them in kind. "You're going to have to do something that might, maybe, hurt someone."

"What?" She still sounded a little out of breath, but the suit was obviously helping more now than it had earlier.

"You see that saucer a little to the left?" Ron pointed to a three man flying saucer currently trying to kill the driver of a sand worm.

"Yes?" She glanced over to Will who shrugged as he ran.

Mai was sure the look had been a question of trust, as in do you trust Ron to just make up a plan without telling anyone. She wasn't sure about Will, but Mai decided right then, she was okay with Ron making things up on the run. He might be a bit of a nut job sometimes but she knew, or rather believed, he wouldn't let them down.

"All right," Ron changed the direction he was running and started heading directly toward the sand worm being attacked by the saucer. "Follow me."

"Ron?" Will asked with more than a bit of anxiety laced in his voice.

"Right," the sand worm was getting closer by the second. "I'm going to toss Lucy up there while Mai shoots the two on the sides. Lucy's going to use the element of surprise to knock the driver out and take over the saucer then come and get us. After that it's zippa-de-do-da-day and through the monolith."

Lucy turned out the be a fairly good driver, especially since the saucer was designed to hold only three lightly armored aliens. The four of them crammed on there, with Ron's armor weighing in as much as an Asian elephant, made the ride a bit lower to the ground than they'd hoped for. As they hit the event horizon around the monolith at speed Mai still had a mental picture of Lucy flying through the air while she was trying desperately to simultaneously hit two moving targets. It was a perfect frozen picture in her mind. Lucy's green and white armor seemed to glow like a Valkyrie against the background of the desert landscape, and under all of it a giant worm with lasers firing from its back. The crowning glory of the shot was, of course, Ron in his blue streaked armor holding his arms up like he was signaling a touchdown in a football game. She could still hear him giggling to himself as the guards yelled and the world rippled around them.

Chapter: Ron

It had been amazing. No, it had been glorious! If there was a better word than glorious he would use that. Maybe majestic, Ron thought to himself. Sand worms, lasers, flying saucers, Mai shooting aliens out of the sky like she was playing Duck Hunt on an old Nintendo. Not just Duck Hunt, but playing it from only two inches away like kids did when they were cheating and wanted to get a better score. She was that good. Lucy had been pretty good too, he had to admit. She'd let him throw her through the middle of all that. Trusting him to get her there, and trusting Mai not to shoot her on accident. A few guards on this side of the monolith were trying to chase them, but Ron knew something would come up, it always seemed to lately.

"Lucy," Will tried to lean forward to talk to her, but the saucer was so cramped that he almost tipped the thing over so he slowly leaned back. "Will this thing stay in the air if you let the controls go?"

"Yes," she looked down at the controls. "Well maybe," she looked back at him, "for a little while."

"Good enough. Bank it around that stand of trees to the right and when we're out of sight everyone jump off. Hopefully it will keep going long enough to crash into that hill and throw them off our trail."

See, Ron thought, something always comes up. They curved around the trees, jumped, and watched the saucer explode in a ball of green and blue fire as it hit the hill. It wasn't a very tall hill, but they'd been flying low so it could have been a big rock and it still would've got the job done.

Crouching under the canopy of what Ron could only think of as a rainforest, he watched Lucy working on Will's side. After some fiddling, Lucy had gotten Will's suit to open from his armpit to his hip. Obviously they'd been designed with these kinds of situations in mind. Lucy had stuck her hand into the tear in Will's jumpsuit and applied some kind of green goo to the injury. "So," Will picked up a stick and watched it dematerialize into his suit, "the next monolith is in the middle of a city, is that right?"

Mai pulled up her holographic display, "Yes," she said. "This world seems to be behind the front lines. The only military activity was back at the base surrounding the one we just came through."

"That's not necessarily true," Lucy said. Ron looked over at her leaning against a tree and wondered, not for the first time, how she was holding up. She wasn't any closer to getting home, and, if his quick research was correct, her home might be in a pretty bad shape.

"Why do you say that?" Will asked.

She looked over at him. With her visor up she looked even more vulnerable, all petite and blue. "Every major city has serious defenses built in. Some are standardized, but others are whatever the local city had resources for."

"Any idea what this place would have?"

"No," she raised her hands and waved at the jungle around them. "I'm not even sure where we are. I know the map gives this place a name, but it doesn't mean anything to me."

"Okay," Will nodded to himself and the jungle. "What about these standard defenses? Any insight into those?"

Shaking her head Lucy looked up through the branches of the canopy. Ron could sense frustration, but he wasn't sure what it was focused on. It could be thoughts of home, or maybe she was feeling particularly unhelpful. If that was the case maybe he should say something since he found throwing her through the air to be very helpful. He watched as Will stepped up and had a quiet conversation with her. Ron wasn't sure if Will was acting in his capacity as commander trying to talk through a problem with a squad mate, or if he was being a guy who wanted to flirt with a blue skinned girl. In this strange situation maybe it was a little bit of both. Looking over at Mai he wondered if he should talk to her. He hadn't really had a chance to find out how she was holding up under the weight of all this crazy, but he decided not to. She looked busy with her little drone.

"Well, suit, it seems it's just you and me." He walked a little way into the jungle. "I wish you had a name. It seems a little rude to just call you suit all the time. It should be something like Susan or Alice." He stopped and pointed to an a bush decorated with orange leaves that looked to be serrated along the edges, "Hey Susan, what's that…" He paused, "Nah, that doesn't sound right. Hey Alice, what's that bush called?"

He saw a quick flash of a menu on his raised visor, but it was up out of his direct line of sight. Then a female voice answered him, "It is commonly known as a Monler, and the barbs on the leaves are highly poisonous. If you touch it with your bare hand you will have approximately three hours before you die."

Jumping a bit backward Ron looked around before stopping himself and thinking it through. I named her, he thought to himself.

I asked her a question… "If you could've talked this whole time why'd you wait till now?"

"This was the first time you have attempted to access those specific set of functions, as well as the fact that some of my parameters were turned off until just recently."

"Well, if you can talk, what do you look like?"

Ron actually felt a sense of confusion, and was reminded his brain was somehow connected to this suit, before a reply came, "I look like a powered suit of armor, which is mainly white but has blue trim in order to signify which class of armor I am."

"Right. That's not actually what I meant, and I kinda thought you could read my mind, so…"

"To a certain extent I can read your mind, but when you ask questions that have no reasonable answer it becomes difficult."

"Right." Ron wondered if everyone could hear her or if he just looked like he was talking to himself. "So I have a question."

"Yes?"

"There's a major city not too far from here with a monolith at the center of it."

"Sranjani."

"What?"

"The name of the city you're referring to is Sranjani."

"Right." He really needed to stop saying that. "My question is regarding the defenses set up to stop us from accessing the jump point connected to the monolith."

"Do you want a list of known defenses, because our intelligence report on Sranjani is fairly expansive since it was a well traveled port before the war broke out."

"No, no, I don't need a whole breakdown. I just need to know the best way to not set them off."

"You must be a registered citizen of Sranjani to use the monolith, and to, as you said, not set off the defenses. If you went in as you are and tried to make it to the monolith many things would either capture you or kill you."

Ron walked back to the group and found Mai continuing to polish Dorothy, and Will still talking to Lucy. Apparently if anyone was going to save them it was going to have to be him. "So, guys," they looked over at him, "I just learned two, no three, very interesting things."

Will stepped toward him, "Awesome, we could use some help here."

Mai let go of the drone which floated just over her right shoulder looking at him. It was a bit creepy. Now that he knew his suit had a kind of personality he wondered what Mai's drone thought of him. "Well," Mai asked. "Are you just going to stand there or are you going to enlighten us?"

"It's just that…" Ron pointed at the drone, "I feel like I'm being judged."

"Oh," Mai looked from her drone back to him, "you are."

"Well…" He looked over to Lucy for some kind of support. That's what medics were supposed to do right? She shrugged at him and waved her hand in that well established get on with it signal. "First," he pointed at the orange leafed bush, "don't touch those with your bear hands. It'll kill you."

Mai rolled her eyes, "And how is that important?"

"Well, they're everywhere around here and I don't know if you're feeling a bit trapped in these tin cans, no offense meant Alice, you might have slipped out of the suit to get some fresh air and found yourself running your fingers through the bushes only to die three hours later."

"Sure," Will said, "and who exactly is Alice?"

"That brings me to point number two." Ron tapped his helmet, "She can talk. I call her Alice."

"You're referring to your suit?" Will asked.

"Yes."

"Mai," Will looked over at her with an implied question.

"Mine doesn't talk." She answered.

"Maybe you just haven't asked her any of the right questions." Ron felt like he needed to defend Alice for some reason.

"It's because," Alice said, "they haven't enabled the correct protocols yet."

"And I did?" Ron said.

"Yes." Alice responded.

"I don't remember doing that."

"You thought about it so I made the appropriate changes. Originally, I wouldn't have been able to, but your field commander turned on the needed access to the appropriate subdirectories."

"Ahhh," Ron nodded then realized everyone was looking at him a bit differently. "Let me guess, you couldn't hear her?"

"No." Will said.

"Here's the deal, you flipped some switches in my suit so that all the bells and whistles would be activated. You remember that?" He

116

looked at Will who nodded back at him. "One of those was the ability to directly communicate with my suit, and for her to have, what appears to be, some kind of artificial intelligence."

"So, kind of like yours then." Mai smirked.

"Ha, ha, and yes," Ron paused then looked over at Mai and smiled. "That was actually really funny and very well timed."

"It's not so funny if you have to point it out." Mai tilted her head and raised an eyebrow at him. She really was pretty, Ron thought.

"Oh," Alice sounded intrigued, "is that why you asked me what I looked like?"

"What?" Ron shook his head, "No, that's not..." Mai looked at him like he was losing his mind. "Sorry, this whole thing about her voice only coming over my suit's headphones is a bit odd. Anyway," he turned back so he could see everyone again, "if you enable the right things in your suits programming, and give it a name, it activates this mode of communication with your suit. It might be faster in certain situations because you don't have to read through the visor display to figure things out."

"True," Will nodded.

"Which brings me to the third thing I just learned."

Mai let out a sigh, "If it has anything to do with going to the bathroom in your suit then I think we can just skip right over that."

"No," Ron added a healthy dose of sarcasm to his voice, "don't be ridiculous. You're the one that needed to figure that out."

"Seriously?" Will shot the question at them both. "Is now really the time?"

"If you can't have a sense of humor Will then I'm worried about you." Ron fired back.

Will raised his hands in mock defeat, "Yes, I get it. It's just..." He shrugged at the entire world and Ron understood.

"I've found a possible way to get to the next monolith," Ron said, "but it will take some improvisation."

The codes had been hard to find, even with Alice's help, but eventually he did find them. Each suit had a designator code that broadcast out to whatever needed it. It was what they used to designate their squad as friendlies. It was what the military establishment used to track you, except in their case, apparently, where no one actually cared where they went. The suits themselves were fairly standard issue on both sides of the conflict because, Ron thought, it was the same company selling weapons and armor to both sides. Gotta make a profit.

Ron had hoped there would be some kind of physical part he could damage so he had an excuse to wander into the enemy camp by the monolith they'd flown through. He just needed some repairs done and could they please put one of their transponder things on his suit, which would then allow him access to stuff. Unfortunately, this wasn't the case. The codes were purely digital. However, when he dug into the suit code, which Alice really didn't like too much, he did find something else helpful.

"Okay," Will said through the communicator, "go over it one more time so we're all clear."

"Seriously?" Mai's voice came over all soft and stealthy and Ron knew she was up in a tree somewhere ready to shoot anyone who looked at him the wrong way. "I understand the whole commander thing, but at this point you're just insulting his intelligence."

Ron liked the fact that bad ass Mai had his back, both physically with a really big sniper rifle and emotionally with Will's over eagerness to be the commander, but in this case it did help him settle his nerves to go over it again. "No worries, Mai." He walked slowly through the forest toward the edge of the enemy camp. "I changed my suit identifiers," looking down at his suit the normal blue glow that outlined everything was changed to green. It turned out the standard suit set up meant every suit had the option to be any color. "I've turned off my broadcast code…" Stepping out from behind a tree he almost ran into a soldier doing patrol. His brain told him he was no good at sneaking while at the same time his suit started to deploy weapons.

"Hey, who are…" the soldier's words stopped at the business end of Mai's rifle.

"Thanks," Ron looked back at the tree tops, "but I might have been able to talk my way through that. It is kind of what I'm trying to accomplish here."

"Sorry." Mai sounded sheepish over the communicator. "A bad guy surprised you and I just pulled the trigger."

"No worries." Ron lifted the downed soldier and draped his arm over his shoulder. "I really appreciate the fact that such a strong and pretty girl is watching over me."

"So let me get this straight," Mai's voice purred over the radio, "You're almost two years younger than me, on a mission in an alien jungle, and you pick now to flirt?"

"Everything okay," Will's voice cut into their private conversation, "or do we need to pull you out?"

"I'm all good." Ron really wanted to keep flirting with Mai, but she was right about the timing. "In fact," Ron picked up the body and staggered forward under the dead weight of the soldier, "I think I can use this to my advantage."

"Wait," Lucy yelled through his helmet.

Ron froze assuming something was about to eat him or shoot him. "What?" he whispered just in case whatever it was hadn't found him yet.

"Your visor." Lucy quieted her voice. "Keep your visor down. Their side doesn't have any humans. They might not recognize you as human, but someone might."

"Right," Ron let out a breath he hadn't realized he was holding, and started walking again.

He would've tried to access this guys suit and steal his identification, but Alice had informed him the suit tends to lock things down very quickly when in the middle of combat. Even a commander doesn't have access to certain functions while the operator is fighting. Ron guessed that made sense. You didn't want some infiltrator being able to turn your systems off in the middle of a fight.

"Ya, hear what happened to the base at Rizon?" The question floated to Ron through the trees from the direction of the camp. He wished he could hear better with his visor down and a menu flickered past his vision followed by Alice's sneaky quiet voice telling him his external microphones had been turned up a bit. Having a thinking suit taking care of him was actually kinda nice.

He wondered if she could become fully aware as an artificial intelligence, which led to the worry that she might decide she doesn't like what he's doing and turn his systems off in the middle of a fight. "Uhm," he wasn't quite sure how to broach the topic with Alice. Did she have any laws of robotics that forbade her from killing the operator of the suit?

"Something happened? I kinda hope it was terrible, with Tod being in charge of a platoon over there." The voice sounded closer this time and Ron adjusted his direction a bit to head toward it while realizing that now wasn't the best time to have an existential conversation with his suit over the definition of consciousness.

"You never did like Tod."

"Well, after he got me trouble for the little poker games I was running..."

"You mean the illegal gambling ring?"

"Anyway, what happened to Rizon?"

"Got tore up by some of those new conscripts from that class three planet."

"Really?" Ron was close enough now to see what the two were doing. A clearly unconscious soldier flopped down between them, dropped there by something that looked like an orange flat bed cart from Costco with no wheels. One of them pulled a metal bar out of a tool box next to him while the other rolled the soldier onto his face.

"Yeah, I also heard the higher ups tried to frag the whole planet to stop them from getting anymore conscripts." He held the metal bar between the unconscious soldiers arms and links extend from it to form some kind of handcuffs.

"I thought it was against the conventions to frag a whole planet?"

"Well, whether it is or it isn't, I heard something stopped them." Heaving together they sat the soldier up and Ron somewhat recognized him. After looking at him for a bit he realized it was the military police officer who'd tried to arrest them back on top of the mesa.

A conflict grew inside of him as he staggered out of the tree line with the very dead soldier in tow. Should he help the big guy or just leave him to his fate? What was his fate? Did they have really nice prisoner of war camps where you got three meals a day and did a little bit of exercise for thirty minutes before sitting around and playing checkers the rest of the time? Or was he scheduled to be recycled into usable organic material and turned into protean bars for the soldier on the go?

"Hey," one of the two noticed him.

"Hey," he said back, "got a bit of a problem here if you could help me with it."

They both ran over to him and the one with the red stripes said, "Is that Dave? What happened?"

"I don't know," Ron replied. "I was headed in for some repairs and," the other soldier came over to his side to help him carry dead Dave, and Ron mentally alerted Alice, "I heard what I thought was a shot. I ran over and found, what did you say his name was?"

"Dave."

"I found Dave like this." A cord quickly extended from Ron's wrist and interfaced with the other soldiers suit. In order to steal someone's identity they first had to be alive, and second you had to be in physical contact with them. The physical contact part was mainly due to the fact that enemy suits wouldn't accept wifi connections from bad guys. Ron couldn't imagine why. Alice dinged at him to let him know one ID had been stolen. Now he just needed to get three more. He'd figured the mess hall would be his best bet. Waiting in line uncomfortably close to another person was just normal at a mess hall.

The commander of the two helped them set Dave down near the unconscious soldier and Ron leaned on him for a moment stealing his ID in the process. Normally this would have been a job for the Gray in the squad. Infiltration skills and the ability to practically turn invisible made stuff like this a lot easier, but the job had been given to Ron because of Alice. "Thanks for bringing him in." The red stripe turned to the other soldier, "Bill, you're gonna need to cover Dave's patrol until I can get back to HQ and send more people over here."

"Seriously?" Bill said. "Man, I'm a mechanic not a grunt, and there's obviously something out there that wants us dead."

"Bill, I am your commanding officer and you do have a gun."

"I got this posting so I wouldn't get shot at." Bill continued complaining to himself as he drew his weapon and headed back the direction Ron had just come from.

Why, Ron wondered, do all these aliens have ridiculous American names. No disrespect meant to the Tod's and Dave's of the world, but how did he make it to the other side of the galaxy and run into an alien named Bill? "It's a translation problem." Alice whispered into his ear making him twitch. "Their names don't fit into your language patterns so I had to make some up from your species file."

"Problem?" the red stripe asked as he punched buttons on a holographic display spreading out from his left forearm.

"Just hungry. Which direction's the mess hall?"

Pointing forward and slightly off to the right he added, "After you get some chow report to HQ so we can take a statement about what happened."

"Yes sir," and with that Ron headed off to see what they had to eat while he probed some aliens for their identities. It seemed only fair.

He really only needed the two he grabbed while he was standing in line, but he was kinda hungry and it never hurt to have backups. He was staring at something that looked like jello when a soldier standing next to him said, "You don't want that. I know it looks like the desert your Ma used to make for you back on whatever planet you're from, but here it mainly just tastes like rotten fish, so take my advice and move along." Ron thanked him and stole his identity.

"You know," Alice whispered, "this is all highly illegal."

Yep, Ron thought, which is why I'm the one here doing it.

"I don't feel like you realize the danger of having an untethered AI living in your suit." Alice continued.

I couldn't agree more Ron thought back while simultaneously wondering if she could hear his thoughts.

"A little bit, yes. It's mainly just impressions I get from your electrical synapses, but the longer I work with you the more your patterns make sense and the better I can read you."

Ron shuffled along and wondered how he was going to eat with his visor down. It flickered along the edge and a half moon shape opened up along the bottom leaving the visor only covering his eyes and forehead as if he was wearing some very large sunglasses. "There are different visor configurations for different species. This one should allow you to eat while still maintaining a basic level of anonymity."

I could get used to this, Ron thought. Untethered or not, you seem to be a nice robot voice in my head.

"You just like me because I'm able to do very illegal things, like stealing enemy ID's to impersonate them while sneaking into off limit civilian enclaves." Alice said.

Back in the forest, it had been determined Ron would be the best choice because he already had his AI turned on, and apparently all of her safety perimeters had been switched off. Will had been apologetic about it, realizing it had been his fiddling around with the base code that had done it. He'd been so caught up in being a commander that he hadn't really stopped to wonder what all of those switches in the code structure had been for. He'd assumed they were like Lucy's where her suit had been limited since she was a medic. Turned out it released a law breaking AI into Ron's suit. It felt kind of like setting a genie free, except Ron wasn't sure yet if this was a good genie or an evil one.

Mai had tried to convince Will it should be her going on this mission, and Will had agreed until Mai's suit refused to steal. Apparently, there were some civil codes locked into their suits and unless you let the genie out of the bottle your suit wouldn't let you do it. Mai tried to convince them it would be in the best interest of the squad to find a way to turn her AI on, but Will really didn't see having two untethered AI in the squad as a good thing.

"You know," Alice said as Ron ate something that approximated a cheese burger, "not all AI are alike and the one they put inside a Gray suit isn't the nicest. They tend to see everything as a target, and the best way to deal with any situation is to shoot it." Ron nodded and Alice added, "And besides, she was still healing."

True, Ron thought, as he took his empty tray to the stand by the door. It was amazing how every lunch room and mess hall throughout the universe seemed to be laid out the same way. He walked out and started back in the direction he'd come from with six new identities in his proverbial pocket when he noticed someone waving at him. "It's the commander from earlier," Alice said. I'll just act like I don't see him, Ron thought, and... "He's coming this way," Alice's voice dropped to a whisper.

Awesome, Ron thought as he turned the first corner he came to. Jogging he turned the next two corners at random just to stay out of the commander's line of sight. Spotting an area where the trees came closer to the buildings, he headed toward it and around the edge of a building just to stay covered for as long as possible. Against the back wall of the building, facing the tree line, the MP Ron had seen unconscious earlier was attached by some glowing blue force to the concrete wall.

Flipping his visor all the way up he made a snap decision, "Hey, you remember me?"

The prisoner's head lifted and looked at Ron. It was hard to read the expression on his face, not because Ron didn't care, but because his face was definitely not human. His skin, or the little of what Ron thought was skin, had a red tint to it, but very little was visible underneath some kind of hard exoskeleton. The first thing that came to mind was rock. It looked like the guy's face was covered in patches of rock. The patches seemed to be random, and for all Ron knew they might be the same as humans getting freckles, or maybe the more rock you had on your face the better warrior you were.

When their eyes met Ron found it slightly disturbing to see perfectly blue human eyes looking back at him. Only so many ways to take in light, Ron thought, but not to himself anymore, now he found himself thinking to Alice. He felt a moment of panic and wondered if she had taken the place of his thinking process.

"You," the military police officer tilted his head, "you're one of the deserters."

"Yep," Ron nodded and looked around to make sure no one was watching, "and the way I see it you have two basic choices. Stay here and let them do whatever they're going to do to you, or..." Ron waved his hands at the restraints, "Come with me and figure things out later. Which is it going to be?"

The officer thought about it and Ron thought at Alice. Can we actually get him free? "In a perfect world where you are just a soldier with a big gun on your back, no." She answered. "However, things have changed since I woke up." Ron worried about her use of the term woke up. That was the kind of term evil, scary things used in the movies, and it made it sound like something bad was eventually going to happen. "There are conventions of war that determine how prisoners are exchanged and normal suit mechanics don't allow for disabling of restraint systems."

Ron waved his hand in the air as a signal to both the officer and Alice to get on with it. He was in an enemy camp just standing around waiting for that wandering commander to find him. "Yes." Alice finally said. "With my digital restraints turned off I can undo the locks on the military police. That is, if you're sure you want him along. The others might not agree with your decision."

The officer took in a deep breath and let it out, "It is against military protocol for an officer to attempt escape, but in this case they have already broken multiple agreed upon ordinances in my treatment as a POW. I accept your offer of help."

"Great." Ron said as he extended his gauntleted hand toward the glowing shackles. A cable extended, just as it had done to steal identities earlier, and a moment later the glowing force holding the MP to the wall disappeared. "Are you armed?"

"They removed my ammunition, but it should be easy enough to replenish it." He bent over and grabbed two handfuls of gravel from the path they were quickly walking down.

"My name's Ron."

The officer glanced over at him, "Crawford."

Once they hit the tree line Ron dropped his visor and started running, following the glowing line Alice drew out for him. He was glad she was looking out for him because in all the twists and turns of this secret mission he'd totally lost track of where their camp was.

"Uhm, Alice?" Ron said quietly so Crawford wouldn't know he was talking to his suit.

"Yes?" She replied.

"Could you send a text message to the squad that I have someone with me? I don't want them, or really I should say I don't want Mai, to start shooting."

"Should I tell them who it is?" Her question seemed to have a hint of laughter in it, or maybe Ron was just putting his worry into her voice.

"Just say I rescued a prisoner that might be able to help us. Wait," he thought about it more, "yes," he added reluctantly, "tell them it's one of the guys who was chasing us."

Chapter: Will

"You did what?" Will was trying very hard to keep his voice to a whisper, not knowing if there were patrols out from the nearby base looking for an escaped prisoner.

"I sent you a message." Ron sulked near Mai who was currently aiming the biggest gun she could find at the new guy's head.

When Will had received the message from Ron, he'd been relieved. He'd been worried that something beyond Ron's control was going to blow up in all of their faces. It wasn't that he didn't trust him to get the mission done, he did, it was he didn't trust this insane universe they all seemed to be living in. For all he knew, the base could have had invisible dragons guarding the perimeter who would have smelled Ron and eaten him before he could do anything. Then he read the rest of the message.

"What, in the name of anything holy on this side of the galaxy, made you think bringing him along would be a good idea, Ron?" Will knew a good commander would find a better, and nicer, way to handle this situation. In fact, all of his training to be a teacher told him to react differently. You should find a helpful way to deal with the bad situation because moving forward he would need Ron and if he tore him up one side and down the other Ron might not be as helpful the next time something came around. Like invisible dragons. On the other hand, the hand he wanted to hit Ron with, teacher training never included alien military police trying to arrest him. And his professors told him all his training was useful and practical.

"Look," Ron waved at Crawford, "he knows his way around. We don't."

"Lucy knows her way around." He looked at her and she waggled her head a bit in a very, I have no idea if this river leads to a deadly waterfall, kind of way.

"Lucy was looking for a way out, just like us. Crawford wasn't. He knows…"

"What I know," Crawford interjected, "is that you're all deserters, and at the first opportunity I'm going to do what is right and haul you in for a court martial."

"Are you kidding me right now?" Ron threw his hands up in the air. "I'm trying to convince my commander not to feed you to the wolves, and you come up with that?" He looked around at the others and his shoulders slumped. "I know he's not very helpful. I know he's actually kind of a jerk. Granted, I didn't know the jerk part till just now. I saved him because it felt like the right thing to do. I didn't know if they were going to turn him into the meatloaf for the mess hall or just ransom him back to the other side, but it didn't feel right leaving him hung up on a wall."

Will sucked in a deep breath. "I need a moment, but…" He looked around and decided sometimes those moments needed to be preempted by the more important, or in this case immediate, things in life. "Ron, pass out the new ID's to the rest of the group. Mai once you get yours please plot us a safe course to the next monolith. Lucy," his side ached and he realized he'd been leaning to the right so his muscles didn't stretch and break whatever seal Lucy'd put in there, "could you please keep an eye on whatever's wrong with me."

He was learning something over these last few hours. It was a lesson life had never thrown at him before. Life before now had been planned and purposeful. Even his most difficult decisions had been well thought out on notebook paper filled with lists of pros and cons. What college should he go to? Days worth of discussion about that. What major should he have in college? That changed halfway through, but he'd thought about it for months. This, however, right now, was just that. It was right now. There was no time to make lists and weigh the choices. He didn't have his normal people around him to bounce ideas off. Sometimes he felt like he was on a river just being pulled along with no way to effect what was happening, but that metaphor didn't feel right. He did have choices. He just had to make them very quickly. That was the lesson. The luxury of time didn't exist right now. Should he take Crawford with them or leave him behind? If he left him behind what would he do? Would he follow them and try to bring them in, messing up their plans at some future point and getting them all killed? If he brought him with them would the exact same thing happen? There would come a moment when the danger wasn't as overwhelming, or maybe they were closer to a base he knew about and Will didn't. Honestly, it would be easier to just have Mai shoot him. She wouldn't argue. Shrugging, she would say it was for the best, and blam, no more problem. But how would Ron look at him after that? Would he even listen to him anymore? And what about Lucy? He craved her good opinion, and he knew it. It wasn't the best situation to be crushing on a blue skinned alien, but sometimes, as he was learning, you just had to make a quick choice and see where the river took you.

That was a terrible mixed metaphor, he thought, then turned to Crawford, "Why do you care so much?"

"What do you mean?"

"I mean, Ron just saved you, we're behind enemy lines, we stopped an all out assault on your position back in that valley, and yet here you are trying to arrest us for no good reason. Why?"

"There is a good reason. You, all of you, were given lawful orders by your lawful commanders, and you disobeyed them. Order needs to be maintained or this entire enterprise will devolve into chaotic groups shooting at each other."

"The problem with your legal defense is that they, whoever they are, are not our lawful commanders, and as such I have every legal right to escape the bonds of slavery that have been placed on me. I was not recruited. I did not volunteer. None of us did. We were illegally kidnapped from our home worlds and forced into labor. You can not, in any good conscience argue that I am legally bound to follow the orders of my kidnappers."

"I.."

Will raised a hand to Crawford's face, "No. There is no argument here. If you think it is legally allowable to kidnap people and force them into service then you are morally bankrupt and therefore I do not need to listen to you." He dropped his hand, "You have two choices, and honestly the only reason I'm giving you any choice is because I trust and respect Ron." He looked over at Ron. Making eye contact Ron nodded his head in thanks at the statement then walked over to Will and hooked to his suit to download the new ID. Will turned back to Crawford, "Choice number one, you come with us, help us get to the nexus of monoliths, then take the enemy maps back to your commanders and present that as your prize. You do no harm to us and you make every effort to help us. Choice number two," Ron unhooked from Will's suit and started toward Crawford, but Will stopped him with a hand on his arm, "you refuse to help us. Any action you take that is detrimental to my squad's safety will be seen as hostile. If you stay here you are saying you will not interfere. If you show up unexpectedly Mai will shoot you, and I doubt you'll survive that."

The number of aliens Will had now seen numbered somewhere in the San Diego Comicon total, and Crawford fell right in with those. His strange carapace of stone, red swathes of skin, and normal human eyes made Will feel like Crawford was just wearing a Halloween alien suit. Staring each other down, Will wasn't even sure what he was supposed to do. It felt like dealing with a wild animal except he didn't know which animal it was. With a black bear you challenged it or it would come after you. With a grizzly bear you quietly tried to slip away. You made and held eye contact with wolves, but never do that with a big cat. What was Crawford? Could he even stare him down or would that signal something romantic? Was Crawford even a guy? Was Lucy even a girl under all that armor? Maybe she was just a head with tentacles coming out controlling the suit.

"Fine," Crawford broke eye contact. "I see no better way forward. I give you my word as an officer I will not endanger your squad, and in return you give me the map to the monolith transportation network to take back to my superiors when this is all done."

Will nodded, not quite sure if shaking hands was even a thing here so he refrained, and turned to the others. "Mai," she turned away from some conversation with Ron, "you got that course laid out?"

"Yes sir." She punched Ron in the arm at the same time as sending the map out to the rest of the squad.

"I'm not part of the…"

Will cut Crawford off, "And you're not going to be until I am amazingly sure you're not going to shoot me in the back. Just be glad I'm letting you keep your ammo."

They kept to the jungle as much as possible, not trusting to the new ID's they'd stolen, but eventually they had to take the road into town. Will had been impressed with all the alien landscapes they'd seen, but at the same time everything had looked strangely similar to home. Trees were mostly trees. The bark might feel a bit different, or the leaves might be a slightly different shape or color. Grass was mostly grass. The world with the giant sand worms had looked an awful like the American south west, minus the giant sandworms of course. Other than the aliens inhabiting them, the worlds themselves hadn't surprised him, and it was a little disappointing. He wouldn't tell Ron this, but he'd secretly hoped for something amazing. There hadn't been, at least as far as he noticed, any worlds with multiple suns. With all their jumps through the monoliths they hadn't seen a night time yet so there's no way to know if any of the worlds they'd walked on had multiple moons. He would've liked to see that.

Walking into the city of Sranjani felt like an extension of any large American city. Some things were different. The cars didn't have wheels. That was cool. But on the whole, it was just another big city. People rode on scooters that could have been a Vespa back home, while others waved for what had to be a taxi. There weren't any other soldiers that Will could see, but he did see a few that might have been their version of police. He assumed, with a military base within walking distance, there would be a lot of soldiers taking leave here in the big city. They would be heading out to the bars to get whatever this alien world's version of Bud Light was, staying out too late, and maybe kissing a girl at the bar who ended up having more tentacles than eyes.

He started humming the tune to I'm Married to a Waitress and I Don't Even Know Her Name. A red line, only seen on their visor readout, lead them through the city. Will didn't leave his visor down constantly because he thought that would look a little off, and might be suspicious in some way so he would check the line, memorize the next few turns then flip his visor back up. Ron, from what he noticed, never put his down, choosing instead to take the city in with as much rubbernecking as possible. If anything about them looked suspicious, it wasn't Ron.

"So, when we get there," Ron glanced over at Mai and Will, "how're we going to deal with the big guns and the force field?"

Mai's visor flipped up and she raised an eyebrow at him, "Do you know something we don't?" She asked.

"No, but that's how stories are supposed to work."

"What does that mean?" She dropped her visor back down and looked at the crowd around them. Will assumed, and hoped, that she was checking for anything that looked like it might try to arrest and or kill them.

"Come on Will, back me up here." Ron watched as a spider legged alien similar to one of the first ones they'd ever seen walked down the sidewalk past them. "In any story, game, or movie, the last waypoint always has some big bad boss to defend it. So I assume there's got to be something there to kill us."

"Ron," Will shook his head, "this isn't a video game. You are correct that things tend to get harder the farther you go in contrived stories, but this isn't that."

Ron shrugged, "At the very least you have to expect the big city monolith headed to the nexus to be defended a little better than the last few."

"They really do stink at guarding these things don't they." Mai said.

"To be fair," Crawford's voice was deep and a bit slow, "they don't expect a small group to do what you all have done. It's not what they prepare for. They expect a battalion to try to take and hold the monolith, not four soldiers to just run through. And what we're doing here isn't protected against at all because it's highly illegal."

"Illegal?" Will saw a prompt pop up next to the red line on his visor asking him if he wanted to review the uniform code of military justice. He dismissed it and saw they had just a few more turns before the plaza with the monolith in it.

"Yes," Lucy's voice was almost ridiculously quiet after Crawford's rumbling base. "It surprised me how stuck on the rules of war both the sides were, and yet how willing they were to kidnap innocent civilians and bomb their cities if they resisted."

"Well…"

Mai held up a hand and stopped Crawford. "I'm gonna do a thing. When it happens that should help us slip through, security or no."

As she turned down an alley, Will saw her report slide by on his visor causing him to smile and nod. "All right," he turned to the others, "I would say to just act natural, but I have no idea what that means around here."

Ron grinned at him, "We're standing in the middle of a large city wearing armor, and I have a giant gun that pops out of my back."

"Exactly," Will couldn't help but grin back at him, "but we need to walk naturally toward the monolith as if we're just normal citizens of this stupid army headed off to wherever they told us to go."

Off to the right, rising above the closest buildings, Will saw smoke. "There's our cue." He started walking, turned the corner and saw the monolith rising from the middle of an open plaza about the size of a football field. It's gray chipped surface belied its reality as a break in the fabric of the universe. Will hadn't taken too much time to examine the last few monoliths they'd used, at the time he'd been a bit busy, but walking slowly toward this one he looked it over. Nothing about it screamed otherworldly alien device. There was no glowing blue light or strange language etched into it. It was slightly larger at the top than at the bottom, but it wasn't carved with perfect angles, giving it a natural look. It was carved, even from here Will could see what looked like chisel marks, which was confusing to him. Why would technologically advanced aliens need to use hand tools to carve out a chunk of rock? There were so many unanswered questions. He was wandering through a mental swamp while it was covered in fog, and every once in a while a flash of light would illuminate something. What was annoying was he never knew what those somethings meant.

Sirens wailed and aliens in various uniforms ran across the plaza. Mai calmly joined them as they walked across the open area. Ron slid over next to her, "You set a building on fire."

"Is that a question?" She continued to calmly walk toward the monolith.

Lucy stepped in front of the pair and walked backward for a few steps, "There could've been innocent civilians inside the building."

Will nodded, and realized he hadn't even thought of that. The only thing crossing his mind had been what a great distraction it was. No one was shooting at them. They weren't trying to crash an overloaded flying saucer through an interplanetary stone pillar, or fighting off most of a military base on their way to a fight with giant sandworms. In his mind this had been a win win, but now Lucy had him feeling all guilty.

"I checked first," Mai said. "There were a few people on the first floor so I made sure to set the building on fire up three or four floors."

"See?" Ron said as Lucy turned back around. "Mai was very thoughtful, wasn't she Will?"

"Actually," Crawford interjected, "the destruction of civilian property in a non war zone is not only highly frowned upon, but in some cases, depending on what the building was, it could be grounds for execution."

They all looked at Crawford for a moment as if they were wondering if he was being serious, and Will noticed that even Lucy rolled her eyes. He wasn't sure what that meant, but he could guess. Here was a member of the military giving a lecture on not hurting civilian structures to a group a civilians his superiors had kidnapped and forced into service. On top of that, if Will had understood some of the side comments correctly, Lucy's home planet might have been severely damaged during the whole kidnapping issue.

Ron waved a finger at Crawford, "Talk about inappropriate. I'm starting to question why I saved you in the first place."

"What?" Crawford looked confused, or as confused as Will could read someone whose face was partially made of stone.

They were interrupted by the presence of the monolith. Since this one was centered in a large civilian space, and relatively unguarded, Will assumed there wouldn't be a military greeting party on the other end. However, you don't survive being kidnapped by crazy aliens by assuming things like that, so he sent Ron through first with orders to clear the way if anything threatening happened. Holding up his hand he gave a slow five count then they all went through at the same time.

We've stepped into an international airport, Will thought. The floor was some form of marble, or at least a reproduction of it, while the walls were a mix of metal, plastic, and glass. There were impressionistic statues that were meant to evoke feelings, but since he wasn't sure what the statue was supposed to be the only feeling he got was confusion. One wall was painted with a mural depicting what looked like a magician putting his assistant into a box and sawing her in half. The group walked away from the monolith, hoping no one was following them after Mai had set a public building on fire.

"Well," Ron looked around, and stepped out of the way of a family trying to pull floating luggage while simultaneously keeping track of three little things running in circles which he assumed were their kids, "this isn't what I expected at all."

Around them, aliens by the hundreds found different ways of getting to wherever they were trying to go. Some rode on floating scooters, others simply walked, while some waited to be picked up by a trolly attached to the ceiling.

If the building was what it felt like, "Look around," Will said. "I expect there's a map close to the monolith we came through to help weary travelers, such as ourselves, find our destination."

The group spread out. Will was certain Ron was actually looking through the shop windows rather than for a map, but he could hardly blame him. It was amazing to him how you could come all the way across the galaxy and airport gift shops would still be selling the same stuff. Shirts with what he assumed were local logos hung on racks next to magazines and snacks. The only real difference was how many arm holes the shirt might have. He was starting to worry about standing out since no one else he'd seen so far had large power armor when Lucy's voice came over the headphones, "The pillar on the other side of the fast food place in the middle of the hall has the map."

They all converged on Lucy's pillar to find the map holographically spread out before them. In shades of blue it showed the building from a top down perspective. Long distance flights departed from the terminals at the top of the map, while shorter flights were going from the terminals on the right. To the left, along with sections marked for maintenance and administration, there was a door labeled with an icon of a red triangle with an exclamation point in the middle.

"An airport?" Mai studied the map. "You have technology that can instantaneously bridge the distance between star systems and you still have airports?" She glanced over at the only two aliens she knew.

Lucy shrugged, "We had two monoliths on my planet. When I was younger our teachers touched briefly on their existence, but we never got into the history or working of them. Like every student I saw them as an amazing mystery, and took time to look up any information on them I could find."

"And?" Mai asked.

"And as far as I could find," Lucy looked at Crawford, "they have always been there, and we have no idea how they work."

Crawford nodded, "It's one of those state secrets that's really not much of a secret. Each government wants the others to think they have it all figured out and could make new monoliths if they really wanted to, however, no new ones have been made in recorded history."

"But what about the story that commander back a few planets told us?" Mai asked.

"Really?" Ron looked over at her with a surprised look on his face. "There's no way that guy's take on any of this was accurate. Not because I think he was stupid or anything. There's no way you get to his rank without being at least a little smart, but that trade and peace relations answer was so educationally contrived that it hurt my feelings."

Crawford nodded, "You must have heard the one about how the monolith network was created to foster a better sense of unity through trade."

The three humans nodded at him.

"Yeah," he shrugged his huge shoulders, "I, as you may have noticed, like to stick to official doctrine." He waved a hand to silence their emotionally loud eye rolling. "I know it's a fault of mine and it's one of the main reasons I haven't been promoted, but we don't need to talk about that right now. My point is, that even I don't believe that story."

"Well, then how do you think they work?" Mai turned back to Lucy, not because she thought Lucy would be more of an expert of monoliths than Crawford, but because she thought he was a jerk.

"The generic belief is that the stones, whatever their made of, act as an anchor. The race that built the network somehow folded space and needed a way to hold things in place after they, in essence, let go."

"No one," Crawford tried to whisper as if the passersby might be listening to their conversation, "can even say what the stones are made of, or even if they are stone. You can't actually get close enough to them to take a sample."

"Right," Ron chimed in, "because when you get close then whoosh," he fluttered his fingers, "off you go to another planet."

"But you do have ships that can travel faster than light." Will said as if that should fix any problems.

"True," Crawford returned to studying the map, "but going slightly faster than the speed of light still takes a very long time to get anywhere. By the time a war ship could get from my home planet to the nearest fighting, more than fifty years would have gone by."

"So," Ron also turned to look at the map again, "I'm guessing it's the door with the danger symbol on it." He pointed to the red triangle then looked up, "Oh, sorry. The mystery of the monoliths and who built them is actually very interesting, I just really want to see what's behind that door, and since the map we looked over back on the sandworm planet showed a hub of multiple monoliths here and I don't see them nicely marked out on the airport map I'm assuming..." He looked from Mai to Will.

"Yes Ron," Will nodded, "you're probably right." Turning to head out Will realized a door with a danger do not enter sign might have some guards, "Mai?"

"Yeah?"

"How're you healing up?"

"I'm fine, Will."

Looking over at her he couldn't tell if she really was fine or if she was just saying that because it's what you're supposed to say in times like this. "Lucy?"

By the time he asked, Lucy had already pulled up a display on her left forearm which he assumed had some kind of health readout on Mai's condition. "Ninety eight percent. The internal damage is all good, and nerve connections are all good. The only thing still healing is some skin at the burn site."

"What?" Mai looked over at Will, "Didn't you trust me?"

"Of course I do. I just thought it would be a good idea to check in with my medical professional before taking your assessment of fine at face value."

"Spoken like a true commander. Also," Mai looked over at Lucy, "how is our commander doing after being stabbed?"

Lucy smiled at this and Will really hoped the rest of her was as pretty as her smile. The thought had re-occurred to him that she might be all tentacles and oozing suckers beneath that cute face, but at this moment he had small hope for anything positive in his immediate future so he chose to hold onto the hope that she was actually gorgeous.

"He'll pull through nicely. The wound is at eight seven percent and shouldn't impede his military readiness."

Will watched Mai nod at Lucy and both girls smile back at each other like sharing some kind of secret. Glancing over he met Ron's eyes and they both shrugged.

Heading toward the left of the map took them past a generic security set up where passengers walked through a tunnel. Will assumed it scanned them for bad things and was slightly jealous that they were allowed to keep their luggage with them, and didn't have to remove their shoes. The fact that some of them didn't have what he would consider feet was beside the fact.

They left the public areas behind and had to break one door handle to gain entry to the side of the airport housing the mysterious door. They were so conspicuous that Will decided to have Ron hack the closest system and turn off the security cameras in the immediate area. He wasn't sure how they'd made it this far without garnering so much as a security guard coming to check on them. Maybe people just looked the other way when big obvious military types walked though. There was a war going on, and if they'd been enemies wouldn't the automatic security system kick in? Maybe, and Will mentally shrugged to himself, they relied too heavily on automated security. Maybe there weren't any actual guards around, and since they'd stolen the identifications just to make it into the city nothing would happen. He still had Ron finish hacking the system. Better to be safe than sorry.

The door in question turned out to be a gray double door with a basic keypad on the right hand side. From the look of it the maintenance crew might use it to access the heating and cooling systems or maybe this is where the flight crew went to hang out. Will would have ignored it and moved on, but it was currently their only lead. If it turned out to be ventilation tunnels for the airport then they would have to reassess their next move, but for now he wanted to know what was behind door number one.

"Ron?" Will gestured to the keypad.

"Right away captain my captain." Ron moved to the keypad by the expedient means of yanking it off the wall and knelt down.

136

Extending a cable and connecting to the pad he started talking to himself, or more likely, Will thought, talking to his live-in artificial intelligence.

Crawford stepped up next to him, "Why are you having your muscle hack the keypad when you have a perfectly fine gray to do it for you?"

Will looked over at him and tried to decide if he was even going to answer. He felt like he didn't need to explain his command decisions to him, but, at the same time, he also felt like he needed to prove to Crawford that he didn't know everything. "Ron's our best when it comes to numbers. He cracked a dead gray's suit security by himself, so we trust him to get it done." He didn't want to tell Crawford that Ron also had the advantage of a suit AI who didn't care about following the rules. Things might turn rough if that came up.

The wall above the now torn off keypad popped open to display an orb filled with twisting strings of light. The light changed color as Ron muttered under his breath, and when it changed again, "I know," Ron yelled at the wall. "What, you think I don't know? Well, I know, and I know you know." Muttering under his breath the cord snapped back into his suit and he removed his right gauntlet. Reaching out gingerly he laid his hand on the orb and started to slide his fingers over it in different patterns.

Mai stepped up and loomed over Ron. Turning her back on him and taking out one of her smaller guns she seemed to look in every direction at the same time. Will was surprised she didn't deploy her drone. For all that, she seemed to keep her words to herself. Will had noticed how her demeanor had changed since they'd first met. Gone was the girl who seemed worried about being shorter than everyone around her, and in her place was a quiet pillar of strength Will could rely on without question. He was also fairly sure she could kick his ass if it came down to it.

A minute went by and he was thinking about asking Ron how things were going, not because it would help, but because that's the commander feeling he got. It was almost a need building inside of him. He needed an update. Ron would understand. It had nothing to do with how much he trusted him, it just needed to be asked. Then, as if to prove him wrong, a click sounded from the double doors in front of him.

"Yes," Ron stood and did a dance. "I am the key master." Grabbing Mai by the shoulders Will thought he was going to try and kiss her, but Ron just grinned and said, "Who's the key master?"

Mai grinned back, "Okay, okay, you're the key master."

"That's right." Letting her go Ron reached out and pulled the right hand door open.

"The question now is," Mai pulled out a larger gun, "who is the gatekeeper?"

The hallway beyond was a tunnel carved from the native rock. With no windows in the airport it had been impossible to tell where they were, now Will was thinking they were either underground or up against a mountain. The tunnel looked rough cut with the curve of the floor flattened out by metal grates. Strips of tape glowed along the ceiling and walls leading to an opening a few hundred feet away.

"Mai," Will's attempted scan down the tunnel showed nothing but tunnel, "could you send Dorothy down there to take a look?"

"Uhm, Will?" Lucy sounded worried, and when he turned to see what she wanted he saw two large robots on tank treads headed toward them. They had a slight military look to them until two large gatling guns popped up on each shoulder, then they had a very military look to them.

"Right," Will headed to the tunnel, "recon will have to be in person. Let's move people. Ron," he looked over his shoulder, "pull the doors closed behind us. Hopefully it'll slow them down."

"Yes sir." Ron replied while waving everyone else though then pulling the doors closed behind them. Will was grateful to see Ron take up the rear position facing the now closed double doors. His back mounted gatling gun and both shoulder mounted rocket pods were pointed at the doors. If anything came though it would get a serious hello.

Will and Crawford took the lead, walking slowly and scanning for anything that might try to kill them. Mai and Lucy were in the middle with Mai looking down the scope on her rifle trying to see what, if anything, waited for them at the tunnel's end. Slowly but surely they exited the tunnel, and looking around, Will realized the tunnel was not part of the original structure. Whoever made the tunnel had simply busted through the wall of what looked like a hallway. The walls were made of white tile and curved up to meet overhead creating an arched hall that curved away rather than going straight. The floor was the same white but gritty, like the floor of a community pool. The tile of the wall was broken where the tunnel had smashed through, and from where Will stood he could stretch his arms out as if to hug someone and the hall made the same shape. It was a sharp enough curve that it was obvious the place made a circle.

138

Will stepped out of the way to let the rest of the squad into the new hallway when a voice sounded, echoing down the empty hall, "Unauthorized clones, you do not have T*gh$^sh@ bl*t#rf permission. Leave Gr*^dlv#old or be destroyed." Will's visor informed him there were translation issues, and he should get a larger sample size so a better translation could be made in the future. At the moment all Will really cared about were two details and they became clear again as the voice repeated the warning a second time.

"Destroyed?" Mai looked around. "By what?"

"Don't say that." Ron popped his glowing shield up and stepped up to cover their left flank. "People say that right before really bad things happen."

"Clones?" Will said to himself. "What does it mean by clones?"

Chapter: Mai

Clones, Mai thought, what's that mean? She scanned the hallway for anything that moved.   Her visor scanning in every imaginable light spectrum, and she was rewarded with movement down the hallway. The wall slid open and something crawled out. A robot about the size of a basketball slid down the curved wall onto the floor. It had six legs and looked like it was made with a kids erector set. No real body or head connected to the legs, just a gun. She beat it to the punch and put a round through it as another one slid out of the hole.

"Uhm, guys," Ron shouted from the other direction, "we've got multiple things coming out of the walls." His voice was overlaid by the sound of gunfire.

More holes opened up on her side and she continued to shoot them before they could get their bearings. "I've got them over here too." Mai yelled back over the sounds of her own rifle.

"Mine just figured out how to put up shields." Ron yelled back.

"Mai?" Will's question floated over the exchange.

"No shields over here." She replied.

"Ron, keep them off us. Everyone move toward Mai."

She wasn't sure about taking point. It wasn't her best skill, especially with her lighter armor and no extra shield, but you do what you have to when the crazy starts climbing out of the walls, so she started moving down the hallway blasting the little robotic buggers as fast as she could pull the trigger. Eventually one popped out with a blue glow around it and Mai's round bounced off and ricocheted down the hallway.

"Mine have shields." She called back.

"Door," Crawford yelled from behind her.

She looked up from the robots to see a metal door off to the right and a matching one across the hallway from it. She watched as Crawford slammed his impressive size into the door. When nothing happened he stepped back and kicked. Again nothing happened. By this time they were taking heavy fire from multiple six legged robots, and Mai was starting to get worried.

"Ha!" Ron's exclamation rang down the hallway. "Vary your ammo type." He called back to them. "If you switch between laser weapons and different forms of conventional ammo you can get through the shields."

The speed with which her suit reacted was amazing. When Ron said it she thought of it and her rifle switched from firing the hard hitting rounds she was using to laser bolts. She couldn't keep it on the same kind of ammo for too long or they would adapt and block it again, so, like Ron said, she had to swap back and forth every few robots.

Pausing from her work creating scrap metal she saw Crawford and Will huddled at the right hand door trying to burn it open with a thin laser on the back of their right hands. With the language coming from Crawford she assumed it wasn't doing anything.

"Keep moving," Will said. "Hopefully there's something up ahead."

As they moved Mai scooped up parts of the robots and turned them into more ammunition for herself. The moving and firing became mundane enough she found her mind starting to wander back in time a few minutes. Clones. The voice in the hall had called them clones. Maybe it was talking about Crawford, or Lucy, but that really didn't make any sense. She wasn't the sci-fi nerd Ron was, and maybe she should just tell him or Will about it and let them deal with it, but she couldn't let it go. Clones showed up in all kinds of movies and TV shows. In reality people had started trying to clone animals and there was even some ethical discussion about cloning a human being, but this was different. This checked all the boxes of her anxiety over the past few days of her life. Why didn't she feel like herself lately? Because she wasn't herself. How did they interface with their suits so easily? Because they were built that way. Her memories of her life before this were all there. Growing up, playing with friends, eating her favorite meal, were all there, but then there was a big blank space and she woke up in that metal room on the spaceship.

"What if I'm not me?" Her finger twitched and a six legged robot died. She swiped over to a smaller faster moving round in her rifle. "What if I died back on Earth." Two more robots died before she had to switch back to laser fire. "Who am I?"

Ron stepped up beside her as the others found another hallway that connected this ring to another. "Mai?" She glanced over at him and his visor flipped up. His eyes found hers through her visor and his voice seemed strangely quiet in the midst of the chaos. "I just met you. You are the only you I know, and this is the you I like." His gun fired and three robots shattered. "We all have past lives, past mistakes, past girlfriends, and boyfriends, and family members we don't want to talk to anymore. I like you, and until something changes and we have a better chance to sit down and think through this, that is all that matters to me. I like you. You are brave and crazy and amazing. You've never twitched or shied away from any of this. You just fought your way through an actual horde of alien robots. I could care less about who you were, or the fact that you were older than me. I like the you that's here now, with me."

She flipped her visor up and met his eyes. Her past self would have cried, but that was before she became, as Ron had put it, a badass sniper. So instead she smiled at him, nodded, and made a mental note to maybe, possibly, kiss him later. Right now, she noticed, the robots were trying to kill them in a new way.

Will and Crawford were actively trying to figure something out, and she could hear them talking over the com system, but at the moment she was filtering them out. She had to trust they would get something done, whatever it was, and in the meantime it was her job to make sure they lived long enough to see that something happen. Earlier, back before they'd found the dead gray at that barn, it bothered her to follow Will's lead. Something inside of her thought she should be independent, that she could take care of the situation better on her own. At first she thought it was just a left over of her previous life. She had been a bit on the introverted side and really didn't appreciate working with, and especially being told what to do by, other people. Now, looking back on those thoughts, she realized it was a little bit of her, but a lot of it was the new programming they'd stuffed inside her new head. As much as she could filter out Will and Crawford yelling at each other it was hard to filter out the fact that she wasn't who she was, or thought she was.

The necessities of life, however, conspired to force her to focus. They, Ron and herself, currently had their backs to a short hallway that connected the first ring they'd entered with another ring. If she remembered the monolith map they'd all looked at earlier each ring should hold four to six of them, but that was the last thing she should be thinking about. The defenses in the nexus had decided the little robots weren't getting the job done. Coming down the left hand curve of the ring they'd exited was a humanoid robot. It's legs reminded her of the prosthetics used by runners who'd lost a leg, causing it to slightly bounce while it walked. One hand, if it could be called that, was a blade and the other was a gun. There was no head and Mai assumed the torso was the location of any sensors that helped it figure out the world around it. The lack of a head made things more difficult. With a human opponent she knew where the logic center, or brain, was kept. On this thing, she had no idea where to shoot for the best result. The layout of the robot made it look as though a badly drawn stick figure was about to try and kill her.

"Ron?" Mai hoped he could just toss a rocket at the killer stick figure and be done with it.

"Uhm, little busy." She looked over to see him bringing up his shield. The gatling gun on his back poked over the top of it and began to spin up. Just around the curve on his side of the ring she saw what looked like a miniature tank, until it stood up.

"Right." She turned back to her problem. Ron could handle that thing. A yell and a crash told her he'd decided to take the fight to the mini tank before it could decide what to shoot him with.

Sighting down her rifle she started taking shots as fast as she could, but it either bounced out of the way or her shots did minimal damage. It leaned forward and charged her. Her finger twitched on the trigger as fast as her brain could react, but eventually the blade on it's hand swung at her head. Raising her rifle she deflected the strike, but noted the damage to her rifle was enough to make it unusable. Using the broken gun in her right hand to continue to parry the blade, her left hand pulled a handgun from a compartment on her thigh. It wasn't a long range weapon so she'd never used it, but it turned out to have a good up close punch. Knocking the blade away to her right she fired from the hip. The energy blast knocked the robot backward, but it managed to keep its feet. If they could be called feet. Before it could react she lunged forward, twisting her torso, and sent a spinning kick at its center of mass with all the augmented suit enhanced power she could manage.

Chapter: Ron

Ron heard a yell from Mai followed by a crash. All his instincts told him to rush to her defense, but that was overridden by a few very basic things. First, there was a giant robot trying to blast his head off. Second, he trusted her to take care of her own problems. She didn't need him coming to rescue her. Come to think of it, it would really be nice if she could come rescue him.

He'd slammed into the robot with his shield knocking it back and giving him a chance to determine the direction of the fight. The problem was the solid base of the thing. It had two tracks that were three to four feet long making it almost impossible to knock over, and it could unfold it's main body to give it a height advantage. At the moment, it was hunkered down using its lower center of gravity to make sure Ron couldn't knock it off it's treads, but when it had been extended the gun on top touched the ceiling.

"Overpower your shields." Alice said, so he did. He wondered why she just didn't do it, but decided to ask her about her personality later. With the extra juice flowing to his shield, Ron rammed the robot again causing sparks to dance across parts of it followed by a few spots of smoke.

A humming sound caused him to look up at the main turret gun where it was glowing red. "Aww, crap..." He hunched his shoulder and braced the best he could but the shock from the blast knocked him back and sent him tumbling into the wall.

"Roll!" Alice yelled at him, and he did one better. Rolling to his left his gatling gun fired randomly in the direction the robot was most likely coming from. After two full rolls, he pushed himself up with one arm while firing a shotgun blast down the hallway with the other. Just to be safe, he followed it with three rockets from his shoulders. Bringing his shield back up, he watched as the robot drove out of the smoke created by his rocket blasts, seemingly unharmed.

"What is this thing made out of?" Ron said while trying to think of something that might catch the killer robot off guard.

"Some of the materials are standard, but there are things which are unclassified." Alice replied.

"It was a bit of a rhetorical statement Alice. However," he fired off a dozen flechettes hoping the supersonic metal spikes might do something his regular bullets couldn't, "if you do happen to see any material that would be easier to blast apart please let me know."

"I think it's quite nice that in the middle of a highly stressful situation you still manage to say please." Alice replied.

"Well," Ron tried to lob a few explosives behind the thing in case its back armor was lighter while deflecting multiple rockets with his shield, "you are…" the rockets exploded on the wall causing him to stagger sideways.

"I am what?" Alice asked. "And on a separate note, this might be easier to blast apart."

A section of the robot lit up on his visor and an idea popped into his head. "Overcharge the shield again," he said.

"Aren't you going to finish telling me what you think I am?" Alice asked again.

"Overcharge the shields now, and we'll have a lovely talk later." His shields crackled with extra energy.

"Just a warning, if you overcharge them again your suits overall power might be compromised," Alice said.

"Duly noted," he yelled as he charge the robot again. The same sparks happened, but this time there were no smoke trails coming from the body of it. He was happy to hear the hum of its main gun again and looked up into the angry red barrel. Tilting his shield caused some of the blast to be deflected sideways, but the majority of it still pushed him backward. Bracing himself against the wall he whispered, "Kaboom." Just as the landmines he'd dropped went off under the tread of the advancing robot. Both treads cracked and his metallic enemy ground to a halt. Now that he'd stopped it, he still needed to figure out what could blow it up. A yell took him off guard and he leaned to his right just in time to see Mai ram some kind of blade into the robot's back. Pulling it out she reached in with her other hand and yanked out a handful of wires.

Chapter: Will

Will's visor was going crazy. The readout for Ron showed damage to multiple systems but no physical injury, while the information on Mai was worse, much worse. They all knew Ron was the tank of the group with thicker armor and that repulsor shield he could throw up, but in these confined quarters Mai had been forced to stand and fight as well. Her left arm shown as broken in multiple spots along with breaks in the matching leg. There was a bullet, or laser, hole going through her abdomen and multiple cuts along her right arm and rib cage. To top it off, literally, her helmet was reporting a concussion with bleeding over her right eye.

He'd already yelled for Lucy, why he made the effort he didn't know, but she was already sending reports back. From the little bit Will caught in the conversation between Ron and Lucy, the robot attacks had ramped up exponentially and Mai had basically saved both of them from very mean toasters.

"Got it." Crawford's voice intruded on his anxiety over Mai's vitals. Focusing back on the problem at hand he saw Crawford toss aside a three foot by two foot panel they'd found on the wall of the second ring. Will had been going crazy trying to figure a way out of this death trap while Mai and Ron held off the waves of attacking robots. Wanting to help them hadn't stopped him from doing what he knew was best for the team, so he and Crawford had continued looking for something to change the status quo. They'd focused on this spot, not because it was labeled as a panel or a different color, but because it wasn't the same shape as the rest of the tiles.

Now that it was pried off, Will could see some kind of computer system. Part of him wanted to finish that thought by saying it was different than anything he'd ever seen, but at this point so was everything else. With Ron and his suit down for repairs, and Mai down for who knows how long, Will extended his hand and had his suit scan for some way to interface with the system. "Crawford, go cover the others while I try and find a way to shut down the defenses." The big man headed back down the hallway without a word, and while Will still didn't trust him he did appreciate his attention to the chain of command.

Finally his suit decided to modify a connector and attempted an attachment to the now bare control panel. Information flooded across his field of vision with, thankfully, only a few words missing because of translation problems. Hopefully those would clear up as his suit received access to more linguistic information.

"Will?" Lucy sounded worried.

"What is it?" He could feel a problem coming just by the tone of her voice.

"Mai's not doing well, and I don't have the tools built into my suit to do the job."

"Right." The map they'd seen in the airport had shown an infirmary, but if they went back out there they were as likely to get shot as taken to the hospital. On the other hand… He shut down everything else and had his suit run a search of the panel's information for a map. In just over a second a two dimensional picture popped up.

"Will," Lucy's voice was strained, "I need something here."

Running his eyes over the map he saw what looked like a medical station at the far side of the next ring. "Ron, I'm sending you a map of this facility. The med bay seems to be just a bit farther on."

"His suit…"

Ron interrupted Lucy before she could finish, "I don't need my suit. Move over." Will heard a grunt then saw Ron, in only his black jumpsuit run by carrying Mai in his arms. "Will, you're going to have to tell me where to go since my visor's not attached to my face at the moment."

Will realized there were two immediate problems. First the systems defenses were still up and running. Not wanting to take the time to properly go through the system he told his suit to find the quickest way to shut them down. While it was working on that, he had to fix the second problem. The door to the infirmary was closed and locked. Finding and opening a single door turned out to be easier than he'd thought. The system wasn't that big, except for the power generating station, and unlocking one door was as simple as flipping a switch. He watched as the medical bay door started to slide up when a chime sounded and all the lights turned off.

"What just happened?" Lucy's voice floated up to him out of the darkness.

A light blinked down the hallway and Will knew Crawford had turned his suit lights on. It was best not to let little death robots sneak up on you in the dark. His suit informed him Ron had been in imminent danger from the system defenses so it had shut the whole system down. This had saved Ron from more robots but had also stopped the hospital door from opening all the way.

"Crawford, go check on Ron. He might need help getting the door open." Now what, he thought to himself.

Lucy's suit began to glow as she stepped up next to him. "Do we even know where these monoliths go?"

Will nodded. Things were crazy, but he could at least do the job right in front of him. "We know one of them goes to the same solar system as our home planet, and another heads off in the direction of your home."

"What do you mean, in the direction of..."

"I mean it would take three more jumps from here to make it back to your home."

She sighed and Will could feel the energy leave her even if he couldn't see her shoulders slump through the armor. "The most immediate problem is gaining access to any of the monoliths. With the power shut off none of the doors will open, but if we turn the power back on..." He let that hang there.

"I'm going to check on Mai." Lucy walked down the now dark hallway.

"Crawford?" Will was hoping for good news.

Crawford's voice came through his helmet, "It seems the medical bay was on its own power source. Mai is, well, something's happening."

"Lucy?" Hopefully she had made it down there by that point.

"They took her out of her suit and laid her on a bed, and now some automatic system is checking her over," Lucy replied. "We'll see what happens once that's done."

Will nodded to himself in the darkness. A good commander would push on with the mission, but he wasn't a good commander, was he. He'd been trying to push this off for as long as possible, and with the death robots, then Mai being hurt, it had been easy to ignore certain things. Now, however, he had to face it. If some unknown alien computer program was right then he, and all his friends, were just clones. He really wasn't sure how he felt about that, or even what to do about it, and maybe that was the point right now. Nothing could be done about it, and thinking about it did nothing to help their current predicament. For a little while he'd been in charge of a classroom, and in that little while he'd said the same thing over and over again to his students. You can't always control your circumstances, but you can control how you react to them.

What needed to happen right now? Mai needed help, and she was getting it, hopefully. They needed to find a way to get through the monolith to home without turning the power back on, because that would just restart the defense systems. What would happen to normal aliens who were supposed to be here if there was an emergency? There had to be something like a fire door, right? There had to be an emergency exit. But where, and how to access it? He could set something on fire and see what happened. Looking around he very quickly realized that idea was a non starter. Nothing in this place would burn, and that had been quickly proven by the fight with the robots.

Doing another quick search of the computer system he saw, again, there wasn't much to this place. There were the monoliths, doors across from them marked with a symbol his suit still hadn't been able to translate, and the power generator in the middle of the next ring. While he'd been worried about his personal existence for a few moments his suit had continued to run through the computer system. He was happy to find there was now a way to turn the power on to some specific areas without turning on the whole place again. These were only emergency systems, like the med bay, and they still couldn't pop open specific monolith doors, but it was a start. The one that caught his attention was the generator room. Emergency crews would need access to that area no matter what happened. Not having a better plan he popped open that door.

"What's up?" Ron padded by almost silently wearing only his black jumpsuit.

"I was about to go and take a look at something. Wanna come?" Will wasn't sure how Ron was doing after the fight, and running Mai down to the robo doctor.

"Sure," Will disconnected from the system and followed Ron down the hallway. "I've got a few minutes while they figure out what needs to be done with Mai." Ron climbed back inside his suit. Will found it strangely comforting to see him back in it. The Ron he knew was a giant in armor, not a normal human walking around in black pajamas. "Alice?" Will couldn't hear the response. "Full system check please. Huh, Okay." He turned to Will, "Seems I used up a good bit of power fighting off Tweedledum back there. Any idea where I might be able to plug into something?"

"Actually," Will said, "we're headed there now."

A short walk brought them to the only open door. Light flooded out of it, and made Will wonder if there was some kind of defense for just that room. As he was thinking about it, he heard something and turned to see Ron warming up his gatling gun and both shoulder rockets. They looked at each other and smiled. It was good to have someone watching your back.

Stepping through the door, Will's mind struggled to take it all in. The door opened onto a platform about fifteen feet across by ten feet deep. A walkway with simple black metal railing extended from the far side of the platform in front of him and stretched out as far as he could see. The room was larger than it should have been. The middle of the ring where this room was housed was maybe thirty feet across, but the walkway disappeared into the distance as if it didn't care about reality. The mind bending size of the room and the simple walkway weren't, however, what was making his brain break. Below the walkway, burning in a magnificent flickering orange was a star. Will's visor immediately dimmed to keep him from burning his vision to nothingness, but the heat of it still pounded him relentlessly. Peeling away from the side of the trapped star was a swirl of corona, twisting like a burning yellow whirlpool and disappearing into a dark spot.

"Well, bad words to that," Ron said, and Will couldn't help but laugh.

"Yes," Will agreed, "many bad words to that."

"Is it just me, or is there a star trapped inside a room being slowly torn apart by a tiny black hole?" Ron asked no one in particular.

"What does Alice have to say?"

"She says it's not possible."

"And yet," Will waved at the sight in front of them.

"You know," Ron said, "all the theories about teleportation, or faster than light travel, end up with one main problem. Not enough power. The human race just hasn't invented something yet that can create enough power to do what needs to be done. This," he waved at the insane sight in front of them, "would get the job done."

"So they harnessed a dying star and used it to power the monolith system."

Ron shrugged, "Maybe that's why no one can build a new one. They don't know how to tap into the power source."

"As cool and crazy as this all is, it doesn't help the situation."

"What's that?" Ron looked at him.

"How to get the door open to our specific monolith." Will looked around the room, which in this case really just consisted of the platform they were standing on. "We need a way to trigger an emergency door response."

150

"Ahh," Ron nodded and started looking around as well. "You think if we do something bad enough the system will be forced to open the doors so we can escape the emergency."

"Exactly."

"So let's make like Hulk and start smashing stuff."

The problem they immediately ran into was the lack of things to smash. The platform they were standing on was surrounded by a waist high black metal railing apparently because they were worried about people falling into the sun. Will worried about that for a moment as Ron leaned out over the railing to check for anything underneath the platform.

"That drone of Mai's would really come in handy about now." Will said as he scanned the walls around the entryway.

"Speaking of Mai..." Ron radioed to Lucy, "Lucy, sweetheart, tell me things are going well."

Will really wished he could carelessly flirt like Ron, but it just never felt natural. He always felt like he was pushing to hard and it would sound forced, or like he was just being weird.

Lucy's voice came back over their helmets, "So far so good, and please don't call me sweetheart."

Will saw Ron wince, "Right, sorry. I'm just trying to deal with…"

"I know." Lucy cut him off.

"How long until we can safely move her?" Will asked, realizing they needed to know that before they caused the emergency they were hoping for.

"She should be able to move on her own in a few minutes, as long as she takes it slow. There's a chance she could re-break something if she rushes it."

Will nodded and his suit beeped as it found something. After his experience in the hallway during the robot attack, he knew there might be a system panel tucked in the wall somewhere. He would say he got lucky, but it was just a good educated guess, and finely tuned scanners. Knowing the process from the last time, he was able to pop the cover off the panel much quicker and found himself looking at the system display for a sun and black hole energy station.

"Ron," he got his attention and Ron trotted across the platform. Will decided it would be better for him to interface with the panel again since his suit already had experience with the last one. He didn't want to take extra time waiting for Ron's suit to figure out how to play nice with the system. However, with Ron's Alice running around in there she might be more willing and able to smash stuff than his suit. "I'll take the first crack at it since I've got experience but if I run into anything I'm going to have you and Alice try to break it."

Ron nodded then, "Can't we both try at the same time?"

Will realized he hadn't thought of that and shrugged. No reason to turn down a perfectly good idea, "Sure." He scooted a bit to the right to make room for Ron and they both plugged into the system.

Chapter: Mai

The vibration of the shrieking siren caused Mai to sit up in bed. The room swam around her as her mind tried to bring her current circumstances into focus. She'd been dreaming about being late to a job interview because she couldn't find her resume. Going from her apartment to an alien medical lab with a siren wailing caused her a nauseous case of vertigo.

"You need to get into your suit," Lucy ran over and yelled over the blaring siren.

Mai wobbled up from the bed she'd been laying on with a head full of questions pressing against the inside of her brain. Where was she? What had happened to the robots? Why was she out of her suit? Was Ron okay? The last thing she remembered was hurting a lot, but knowing she had to kill the robot going after him. If anything was going to shoot Ron it was going to be her. There was a vague memory of someone carrying her and the lights going out, but it was all hazy and distant.

"Mai," Ron slammed into the door as he tried to take the corner at full speed, "we have to go now! Now, now, now, now," he was reaching for her as if he was going to grab her and run, but she didn't want to leave without her suit.

For a moment, as she stumbled toward open back of her armor, the siren stopped and a voice came on, "Gravitational containment failure. All employees report to assigned lifeboats." The message repeated another time before the siren came back.

"Ron," she looked at him as he helped her into he suit, "what did you do?"

"Well," her feet settled into her boots, the suit closed around her, and his voice started coming over her headset, "there was a star with a black hole powering the monolith jump points and Will and I kinda broke it so we could get outa here."

"Severe gravitational anomalies detected." Mai could hear a female voice coming over the headset and it wasn't Lucy.

"Who's…"

"Yes, Alice," Ron said. "We set a black hole loose. I expect there will be all kinds of anomalies. Let's just get to the lifeboat."

Mai started running in the direction her visor was showing but the pain in her leg caused little sparkly lights to dance in her vision while the world seemed to head down a shrinking tunnel. Ron caught her and suddenly she seemed to be flying down the hallway. Glancing around she realized they were flying, as her visor informed her gravity had become somewhat optional. Hearing Ron's boosters fire she looked down the hallway and saw Will waving for them to hurry, and then Will was gone and it was Lucy waving at them. Then somehow both Lucy and Will were there at the same time. Ron said something, but it was like a warped recording, all distorted and wrong, sounding like someone had speed him up too fast. She tried to respond but stopped when the floor started to stretch away like some at the end of the hall was pulling it like taffy.

Ron's feet hit the ground at the same time as he said, "That was nuts." Up ahead, Will waved them toward an open door. "Will," Ron set her down at the door, "I think we broke the universe."

"Nah," Will replied, "just this little part of it. Now, get strapped in."

The lifeboat was essentially just that and Mai had to squeeze to fit in next to Ron. She wasn't sure who the aliens were who built this place, it seemed no one really was, but they weren't the size of her powered suit of armor. The ship was basically the size of a family dining table with seating for six, except in this case it was five with really bulky clothes. Will and Crawford were in the front presumably because Crawford might actually know how to fly a spaceship if it came to that, and Will because he might need to keep Crawford in line.

Once they were all in, the top of the ship closed and video screens flickered to life around them. It made sense not to have windows of any kind. If there really was an emergency large enough to evacuate a place like this you wanted your ship to be as secure as possible, and windows were just asking to get broken. The screens showed the door in front of them and the monolith across the hall. According to Will's continuing explanation this one was the way home, or at least that's how he'd read the map. The ten foot stone monolith started to stretch and twist. The stone surface bending and elongating itself into a bad example of a mobius strip. Distance and even her perception of reality became fluid with Ron being replaced in the seat next to her with Lucy then with a green skinned alien she'd never met, but felt somehow like she knew him, then back to Ron. At the same time red lights on the dash blinked out one by one.

"Uhm," her head hurt just looking at the world around her, "should we really be going through a wormhole while that's happening?"

Ron, or Lucy, or somehow both at the same time, looked over at her, and depending on who it was in the moment either took her hand or smiled reassuringly. Will looked over both his shoulders, "Hang onto something."

The last red light blinked out and the ship launched forward with such instantaneous force Mai worried her list of injuries would soon include whiplash. There was a moment of gut wrenching vertigo unlike any other time they'd been through the event horizon and jump point of a monolith, followed by stillness. The screens showed blackness or were simply off and everyone seemed to hold their breath waiting for the next catastrophe. Granted, if what Ron said was true, they'd been the cause of the most recent one.

"Well," Mai said, looking over, not quite sure who she was going to see and happy it was Ron, "you can add breaking the universe to your list of accomplishments."

Ron laughed, then Will laughed. Mai was fairly certain Lucy was laughing but there might have been some crying in there as well. Crawford did something that could have been a laugh, but she wasn't sure. "And that," Ron's visor was up and that giant grin of his was shining on her like the sun, "is why I love you Mai."

She leaned forward and gave him a light kiss, "I love you too."

The silence was embarrassingly long and Mai cleared her throat just to break the spell. Will reached forward and pushed a few buttons, maybe just to see what they did, and said, "So, does anybody know how to figure out where we are?"

Mai tried her best not to think of what was currently happening to the airport they'd just left behind. Everything had happened so fast, and she'd been unconscious for a good portion of it, but she really hoped there was something built into that place to contain whatever Ron and Will had done. All those people standing in line to catch a flight. What would that be like? Looking forward to getting home for Christmas, or whatever they had that passed for Christmas on the other side of the galaxy, only to have a black hole tear a hole in your world.

After a few minutes of Will fiddling with the controls the view on the screens shifted to show a star in front of them and what looked like rocks floating in the nothingness of space behind them. "So here's what we've got so far," Will said from the front seat. "We seem to have exited the monolith on the dwarf planet Ceres in the asteroid belt. For those of you either not up on your astronomy, or just not from this solar system, our planet, Earth, is a couple planets closer to the sun from here. Our current velocity is fairly staggering. Those guys weren't kidding when they set up this evacuation."

"I guess," Ron had taken his gauntlet off, and after giving her a look she took hers off as well, and was holding his hand, "they weren't sure if the emergency would cause the system to blow up, possibly shooting who knows what kind of energy and radiation out, and wanted people as far from them as possible?"

Mai liked the fact that she liked him, and she liked the fact that he was smart, but what she really liked best was she'd saved him, not the other way around. Sure, he might have been able to take the robot out on his own, eventually. That wasn't the point. The point was, for her whole life, up till now, she'd been a short Thai girl. That was it. That was the defining characteristic of her entire life. All through high school and in all her relationships or just friendships, the standing joke, pun intended, or statement was her height. Now, no one cared how tall she was because she was the badass sniper, because she saved Ron from a giant killer robot. Holding his hand was nice, but it was better because she knew, if she wanted to, she could take him down.

Chapter: Will

Will finally found the right series of buttons. It would've taken longer but his suit had some experience now with the strange language of the monolith builders. The problem ended up being, not that he couldn't read the language, but the aliens had designed a really poor interface. He had to go through three different menus and submenus to find the controls for the thrusters. They were going at an amazing clip away from Ceres, which had dwindled to nothing very quickly, but they needed to be going faster to get to Earth in a reasonable amount of time. At any other time their speed would have been something to proudly note down. This had to be the fastest any human had gone. However, there was only so long they could be this cooped up on the lifeboat before running out of food and air. Their suits had a small supply of air, and the lifeboat seemed to be able to recycle the breathable air, but he didn't know how long that would last, and getting on the ground as quickly as possible would be preferable.

With the thruster control ready and waiting, he hesitated. He didn't want to just push them forward as fast as possible when forward might be the wrong direction to go. He needed to know where Earth was, and where it was going to be, so he could get them going in the right direction. "Ron?" They'd turned off their suits com systems since they were packed shoulder to shoulder. With them on, it created an annoying doubling of every sound.

"Yes sir," came the response from the back seat.

"You think you could hook up to the ship? If I remember correctly it was your part of the map that showed our solar system, and I was hoping for something useful to get us going in the right direction."

"I'll give it a try, Admiral."

Mai's voice was quiet without the help of the suit com system, "Admiral, really?"

"What?" Ron said. "We're in a ship now. I thought it was appropriate."

Will shook his head and looked back to see how Lucy was holding up. She gave him a weak smile and he wished he could talk with her about everything but the close confines, and the necessity to look backwards, made it difficult. He knew she must be sad about missing her chance to get home, and he made a promise in his own head that he would continue to try no matter what.

When he turned back around the monitor in front of him was showing a top down version of the solar system. The direction and speed of each planet was listed next to them. "Wow, good job Ron."

"Don't thank me, thank Alice."

"Well, then tell that very helpful artificial person in your suit thank you." Will mentally plugged their location together with the location and movement speed of Earth into his suits computer. A few seconds later a heading and speed was ready. "I love alien technology."

"After everything we've been through?" Ron said.

"When you put it like that…" Will punched in the heading and turned up the thrusters to max. "We should be in sight of Earth in five minutes."

"Five minutes?" Ron's voice was the definition of incredulous.

"Like I said, at this moment, I love alien technology." He knew from the general readouts that they were going over two hundred and fifty seven million miles in around five minutes. His suit caught his thoughts and popped out the speed of light at one hundred and eighty six thousand two hundred and two miles per second, which would mean they were doing roughly twice the speed of light. No big deal. Just going faster than the speed of light. In a tin can they just shot out of an exploding wormhole pinned down by an alien monolith. Will watched the readouts as they flew through the space between Mars and Earth. He was bummed they didn't get to see Mars, but it was currently on the other side of the sun, and at their speed it would've been nothing but an elongated blur. He was just glad Earth hadn't been on the other side of the sun.

A few minutes later the screens showed a pale blue dot growing with each passing second. Eventually the moon became visible and Will started to wonder how they were going to slow down. He put directions into the ship's computer and thrusters of some kind kicked in to slow them from going faster than human physics said should be possible to just unreasonably fast. It wasn't slowing down enough. This was a lifeboat so it stood to reason it should have a way of landing. He started, as quickly as possible, going through the terrible user interface looking for the landing procedures. "Guys," he read the screen and sighed, "I have some bad news."

When they entered the atmosphere small thrusters on the nose of the lifeboat fired to slow them as much as possible, but they had run through most of whatever counted as fuel trying to speed up and make it here, then trying to slow down so they didn't fly right by. This meant the small landing thrusters weren't going to be much help. That was followed by large metal panels popping out from the sides and acting as air brakes. The vibration of the ship rattled Will"s teeth at a frequency he was sure would cause them to shatter spontaneously until a metallic screeching followed by a nauseating spin informed him something had gone wrong. The ship seemed to be screaming and Will wasn't sure what to do if things went horribly wrong and everything broke. Would their suits be good enough to survive a crash of this magnitude, he wondered. Would their new enhancements keep them alive even though they were broken beyond repair? Finally a blinking warning on the display was followed by a massive jerk as a parachute deployed, attempting to slow them down the rest of the way.

Whoever had designed these lifeboats had not thought this whole process through, Will decided. Either it was done by a bidding war to see who could land people for the least amount of money while technically keeping them all alive, or the aliens who built the monoliths just were tougher than humans. What all of this felt like was the world's worst maintained carnival ride kept changing its mind on what it was trying to be.

Eventually their speed was low enough for small flight wings to deploy from the sides allowing them to go from a nose dive to more of a flat incline for the inevitable, because again the design was insane to Will, crash landing. Once the ship had settled into the dirt and the worrying popping noises subsided he pushed the button to open the main hatch. Will wasn't sure what would be there to greet them when they came out. After the giant alien spaceship had shown up over Earth, and millions of people had been kidnapped, he suspected the nations of the world would be less welcoming of another alien artifact falling from the sky. As the hatch opened he expected to see soldiers, or helicopters with large guns pointing at them. When it finally opened he was very surprised. Empty desert sand extended in every direction without a soul in sight.

Piling out of the cramped lifeboat they all took a moment to stretch. Will's visor popped down automatically to shield his eyes from the sun. "Mai, could you send Dorothy up to have a look around, please."

The little drone leapt into the sky and a few seconds later Mai turned to him, "Will," her voice seemed a little off Will thought, and that worried him, "you need to see this." She pointed in the direction Dorothy had flown and they all started walking.

Cresting the top of the closest dune Will's mind froze on the image in front of him. Rising from the desert next to a ribbon of water was a giant pyramid. Its sides were clad in glimmering white with its tip shining gold like a second tiny sun. Next to it he could see thousands of people crawling over a half finished second pyramid. Zooming in with his visor he could make out groups of people dressed in white loincloths pulling huge blocks of stone over rolling logs.

"Will," Ron stood next to him pointing at the scene, "that's…"

"Yep," was all Will could think to say.

"And they're not even done building the second one so that means…" Ron's voice trailed off as they watched Egyptians build the second of the three great pyramids.